D0006361

# Mary Wine

# Alcandian Quest

Ellora's Cave
Romantica Publishing

An Ellora's Cave Romantica Publication

www.ellorascave.com

Alcandian Quest

ISBN 1419902172, 9781419952807
ALL RIGHTS RESERVED.
Alcandian Quest Copyright © 2005 Mary Wine
Edited by Sue-Ellen Gower.
Cover art by Syneca.

This book printed in the U.S.A. by Jasmine–Jade Enterprises,
LLC

Trade paperback publication April 2005

With the exception of quotes used in reviews, this book may
not be reproduced or used in whole or in part by any means
existing without written permission from the publisher,
Ellora's Cave Publishing, Inc.® 1056 Home Avenue, Akron OH
44310-3502.

Warning: The unauthorized reproduction or distribution of this
copyrighted work is illegal. Criminal copyright infringement,
including infringement without monetary gain, is investigated
by the FBI and is punishable by up to 5 years in federal prison
and a fine of $250,000.
(http://www.fbi.gov/ipr/)

This book is a work of fiction and any resemblance to persons,
living or dead, or places, events or locales is purely
coincidental. The characters are productions of the author's
imagination and used fictitiously.

# ALCANDIAN QUEST

# Chapter One

**ဩ**

"Come on, Jessica, don't be so medieval. It's the twenty-first century. Come over here and have a little fun with me. I've been a good boy and waited for you."

Jessica lifted her eyelids to stare at her boyfriend. Bryan palmed a naked breast in his hand as Jessica's girlfriend, Gwen, giggled with delight. Heat hit Jessica in a wave as she watched the two touch and caress each other.

Bryan was a good lover. Finding out Gwen knew that little fact from more than secondhand information made Jessica set her jaws stiffly together. But her eyes were glued to Bryan as he licked one of Gwen's large rosy nipples. His tongue flicked back and forth across the girl's flesh, making Jessica shift as her own nipples tightened.

"Jessica, we're friends, let's not fight over a man." Gwen batted her long eyelashes. "It will be so much better to share him."

"Umm, I want to be shared." Bryan raised his blond head to give Jessica a wink before Gwen pushed him onto his back. He laughed as his body landed on the bed's overstuffed pillows.

But it was *her* bed. *Her* tiny townhouse, *her* girlfriend and what Jessica had *thought* to be *her* boyfriend. Well, tonight was certainly turning out to be a newsflash.

Gwen came up on all fours like a sleek house cat. She purred loudly as she nuzzled Bryan's erection. She rubbed her cheeks against the hard staff before she began to lick it with delicate laps.

Bryan's face became a mask of enjoyment. Jessica found her eyes glued to Bryan's face as the sound of Gwen sucking on his engorged cock hit her ears. Bryan loved to be sucked off. Gwen seemed to know that little fact just as well as Jessica knew it herself. The other woman wrapped her fingers around his swollen cock and took the entire head between her lips as her fingers stroked the remaining length.

"Oh yeah, baby...take it all."

Jessica felt her passion die as Gwen's little kitten sounds hit her ears like someone scraping the surface of a chalkboard. All that rippled across her skin was the need to make a quick exit. Bryan's fingers twisted in Gwen's hair as his hips thrust his cock deeper between her lips. His eyes opened to watch his erection disappearing into Gwen's mouth as his lips twisted into a smirk.

"Jessica can take more and suck twice that much."

Gwen immediately increased her efforts as Bryan chuckled at her. His eyes rose until they found Jessica. "Come on, Jessie, I can't wait to fuck you both."

Jessica turned on her heel. Leaving her own home was rather strange, but there was no way she would be joining the party.

That didn't mean she was a prude.

Slamming her car door, Jessica turned the engine over and punched her foot onto the accelerator.

It wasn't even the idea of a threesome that had driven her out of that bedroom. It was the very cheap look that Bryan had cast onto Gwen's lowered head. How did a man let a woman suck his most sensitive parts and not look like he respected her?

Bryan did like her. She had been considering listening to her heart instead of her head, and taking their relationship to the more intimate level that he desired.

Instead Jessica headed for the interstate. It was Friday night and she was driving up to the mountains for the weekend. Crestline would be beautiful this early in spring. It would also be brisk, but maybe a little cold air would cool her blood down. Besides maybe the serenity would help her discover just where she'd mistaken Bryan for a man she might be willing to marry.

The miles dropped behind her jeep and as they did, so did the tension. Jessica felt her lips twitching up into a grin as the mountains came into view. Her parents had retired to the California Mountains, but the harsh winter conditions made the couple reconsider and they had moved to the warmer city of San Diego. The large A-frame house they'd bought was as close to perfection as Jessica thought a house could get.

So, she'd bought it from them and never once regretted the pinch it placed on her budget. Right now, she could only escape her tiny city apartment for the cabin when work permitted. But her dreams held a future where Jessica would join the growing number of telecommuters and be able to move to the mountains completely.

*Ah, damn it!*

Why did she always pick a dog? What was it about the word *relationship* that made it so tough to find a guy who wanted both the sex and the attachment? Maybe the problem was with the word—guy. What Jessica needed was a man.

Well, Bryan was a guy. A cute guy who was living every other guy's fantasy tonight. He was getting laid. Jessica had always considered that phrase vulgar. She didn't want to get laid. She wanted to make love—hot, passionate intimacy that would tear into her soul. The kind of embrace that would fill her heart, not just her body.

It looked like she was the one fantasizing now. Still, of her two choices, the fantasizing felt better. Sex was something she wanted, but without a relationship, she just couldn't see offering that one secret part of herself to any man. Bryan's words floated across her mind as she considered his plan to pit her and Gwen against each other in some kind of twisted competition of oral sex skills. Jessica didn't mind being his toy in the bedroom from time to time but that kind of play came with becoming a man's partner outside the bedroom walls. Without that, sex was an empty illusion of intimacy.

Maybe she'd call Bryan tomorrow and thank him. She couldn't even squeeze out a single tear for her now ex-boyfriend and Jessica hated wasting her time on anything or anyone.

She slowed down as she entered the forest. The roads were narrow and in the dark you could drive right past your turnoff if you didn't pay attention. The road in front of her was coated with a fine sheet of frost. Her headlights made the ice glitter with a thousand multicolored lights.

Spotting her turn, Jessica headed her jeep up the driveway that led to her cabin. A smile lifted her lips because it was good to be home. She opened the garage door with a remote control and pulled smoothly into her parking spot. Another jab on the remote control sent the door down behind her taillights.

Jessica squealed as she opened the car door. It was nippy tonight! She shoved the door closed. The garage was the bottom floor of the house. The living area was above her and so was her jacket! It was a darn good thing she kept extra clothing at the cabin because she hadn't even thought about grabbing anything on her way out of her apartment.

Rubbing her arms, she hurried up the steps. There was a door at the top of the steps that helped keep the heat in the house. Giving the knob a quick twist she leaned her shoulder into it. Warm air hit her arms, the contrast with the frigid mountain air made her freeze in her steps.

There was a ruby glow filling the living room. A bed of glowing coals sat in the fireplace, filling the room with heat. Fear tried to bloom into panic but Jessica resisted the pull. Someone had been in the house, if they were still there. She needed to keep her head.

The glow from the fireplace left too many dark shadows. Inching forward, Jessica reached for the light switch. Her wrist was brutally gripped and her feet jerked right out of their tracks. Jessica threw her weight into the fall to reverse the hold on her wrist.

She twisted and lunged, sending her assailant tumbling over his own arm. She tightened her grip and twisted the wrist she held with all her strength.

"Argh!"

"You aren't going anywhere, buddy." Her voice sounded far steadier than she felt. Jessica considered the phone, but it was too far away to reach. She wedged her knee against her captive and felt the hard layer of muscle his shoulders were coated with.

Great. She had him all right, but they couldn't exactly spend the night like this. A soft grunt hit her ears a second before she was surrounded by another of the room's shadows. A squeal escaped her lips as she was lifted clean off the floor, turned and clamped against a body that was huge compared to her own.

Flinging her head back, Jessica struggled to see in the room's meager light. The dying coals washed over a harsh jaw that was angled towards her face, a blue flash crossed his eyes making her blink and stare at his face in confusion. She was smashed against the man's chest and she didn't think her feet hung past his knees. She was horrified by the sheer size of him.

Jessica felt her jaw drop open. People's eyes didn't flash. Fear must be making her crazy.

"Put me down."

"Do not. She is wicked."

His eyes flashed again. This time they were silver-blue, but still electric. "She bested you fairly, Caius. She evoked no foul play."

A low growl was the reply. Jessica took a glance over her shoulder to see the tall shadow of the first man. He raised his arm and shook the wrist she'd been twisting. He growled again as he flexed the fingers.

Her captor's eyes flashed again as he angled his large head towards her again. Time froze in that second. The room spun around her as her eyes became focused on his face. He burst inside her head like they were the same person. She became aware of his pleasure in their embrace as keenly as she knew that her own body enjoyed being next to his.

Light flooded the room. Her captor turned with her bound to him to face the far light switch.

"Jessica? What the hell are you doing here?"

Jerking her head around, Jessica felt relief slam into her. Her temper followed right on the heels of that emotion. Her brother was leaning against the doorjamb, wearing a robe that was falling open because he'd obviously just tossed it over his nude body. Cole gave her a harsh look as he jerked the tie around his waist.

"Do I need a reason to come to my own house?" A low rumble shook her breasts. Jessica snapped her attention back to her captor. His eyes flashed again, now more green than blue and his lips widened into a smile as he inspected her face. He didn't miss a single detail. Jessica felt her breath lodge somewhere inside her throat as his dark eyes probed hers.

"Put me down." Her demand sounded more like a plea. Color rushed into her cheeks but Jessica didn't care. She wanted away from him…right now.

A single dark eyebrow raised on his wide forehead. The need to struggle bubbled up inside her, making her tremble. His lips softened in response to her body's shiver, but his arms bound her to his length with no hint of release.

His eyes returned to hers as he lowered his head slightly. His eyes closed to mere slits as he sniffed her neck with a deep breath that made his chest rise in a fluid movement against her body. His eyes opened wide as they flashed silver-blue again. Alarm raced down her nerves. Jessica was quite certain no one had ever deliberately smelled her. The action hit her as highly sexual and it sent a tiny curl of excitement towards the deepest part of her body.

"Is she your woman?" Now that was a demand. His voice was a deep rumble that bordered on a roar.

"My sister. Put her down before she kicks you with that foot. Trust me, Jessica knows what to aim for and how to hit it right."

Her captor shifted his hold at near light speed. Her brother's words were barely out of his mouth before one solid arm slipped down her body to clamp over her thighs. She'd raised her right leg up in order to deliver a solid groin shot to him with a good thrust from the side of her foot. Now she was clamped to his hips with one leg around his waist. The curl of heat that had started in her belly was now burning along her sex as she was spread open against his body. The horrible part about that was the fact that her body seemed to almost sigh as the folds of her sex separated. Her body didn't listen to a single rational thought, instead it softened and melted against the hard male body.

"Cole!"

"Do not be angry. I like my man-parts the way they are." His voice was a deep rumble that he softened as he aimed the comment at her ears. His fingers actually petted the cheek of her bottom gently in a soothing motion. A deep strength seemed to seep through the thin layers of clothing separating them. His face lit with amusement as Jessica glared at him. He was enjoying watching her. More heat rushed into her cheeks in response.

"That's my baby sister, Dylan."

The chest she was smashed onto shifted and rubbed against her. Jessica gasped as her breasts felt like they were being petted. The nipples lifted slightly as he rubbed against her a second time. It was a deliberate movement, his eyes watched hers, making sure she noticed that the touch wasn't accidental.

Her feet hit the floor a second later. Jessica jumped away from the man with her arms coming up defensively.

"Sister, yes. That is written on her face." The blue flash crossed his eyes as he dropped them down her body over each curve. "However, she is a woman. Not a baby. Not even a girl. She is fully mature."

Jessica stared at him in astonishment. Had he really just given her the once-over? Right there in her living room, in front of her brother? For that matter, the first man she'd come into contact with moved forward with a deep scowl aimed at her.

Jessica let a smug smile lift her lips. No one mugged her! But this wasn't a full-grown man. She considered his face. Although he possessed the same hard jaw angle, his smooth skin betrayed his youth. His face hadn't set into the hard line of manhood yet. Still, he stood a good half-foot taller than she and outweighed her.

Cole's friend was certainly a man. She stared at his eyes and discovered them to be jet black but flashes of blue seemed to cross them almost like a current of electricity. To go with those eyes, he had black hair, longer than she was used to—the tips just brushed his shoulders. A thin braid pulled his bangs away from his eyes, and was cast behind one of his ears. There was something intense about him. He was huge—somewhere close to seven feet of pure muscle. His wide shoulders were packed with thick muscles and Jessica let her eyes linger over his form because she'd never really seen a man that muscular except on the fitness magazine cover at the supermarket checkout. His body fat had to be almost nonexistent.

"Do I meet with your approval, *darmasha*?"

"My name is Jessica." The words fell out of her mouth as she tried to stop gaping at him. Lord! It really wasn't her night!

"That is our word for an honored female." He said it like a lesson that she was expected to remember. Jessica let her eyes return to his chest because his clothes were odd. She might have even labeled them a costume but they didn't look flimsy like most fantasy outfits were. His pants were deepest black, but not made of denim. Instead it looked like some kind of thick, natural leather. They were molded over his legs and tapered down his calves where boots laced up over the pants. He wasn't wearing a shirt, but rather a jacket of some type that fell three quarters of the way down his body. The thing was crossed over his chest, leaving a deep neckline that displayed some of those muscles. Slits ran up the sides of the jacket all the way to his waist. The way he stood made his legs visible through the slits. The coat was made to allow for any movement he might choose to make.

"Jessica, you should have called me." Her brother was still grouchy. Jessica turned on him because she just had the notion that she had a better chance of winning against Cole. His friend was making her…nervous.

"Excuse me?" Jessica propped her hands on her hips as she faced Cole. The man behind her chuckled. Actually he laughed, in a low, male tone that made her face explode with heat. It took every ounce of willpower she had to keep her eyes on her brother.

"Last time I checked, I was the one paying the mortgage on this house."

Cole's face relaxed as he let a grin lift his lips. Her brother was too handsome for his own good. The result being, he was spoiled rotten when it came to women. Jessica knew for a fact that the only other woman on the planet who dared to put Cole Somerton in his place was their mother.

"Sorry, Sis. I forgot you run up here on the weekends. I needed some place discreet."

His voice deepened. Jessica knew the tone. Cole wasn't…well…normal. She'd learned a few years ago to not ask a whole lot of questions about her brother's rather reclusive life. His companions tended to be dark and hardened.

Most importantly, they tended to be armed. That explained his need for someplace discreet. Tipping her head back around, Jessica considered her brother's...guests. She couldn't put her finger on just what it was about them that was screaming at her. They were certainly foreign.

The larger one's eyes were glued to her in some unspoken quest. She was oddly aware of the man and even her skin felt hypersensitive to his stare. Those black eyes dropped to her breasts and Jessica barely kept her gasp inside her mouth. Her nipples actually tingled under the weight of those black probes, the little nubs rising and tightening with sensation that flowed straight down to the folds of her sex. Once again her body began to beg for her to shift her thighs apart and open for him. He raised his head in a flash to peg her eyes with his. A smug grin lifted his firm lips. Jessica pressed her own mouth into a tight line. There was no possible way he had any clue that her...nipples were...tight.

"Well...that's that...I guess." Jessica turned back to Cole. It was almost a defensive move. His companion was just a little too extreme for her to deal with. "I'm beat."

Cole nodded his gratitude at her. It was a hard expression that she knew he didn't grant to many people. Cole didn't lead a soft, civilian life. Jessica made sure to remind herself of that fact when little things, like tonight, happened. Cole was working on something that she was better off not knowing any details about.

And she loved her brother enough to turn a blind eye. "'Night."

* * * * *

The phone began buzzing at exactly eight the next morning. Jessica grabbed it and muttered as the cord tangled around her hand. She ended up dragging the entire thing off

16

the bedside table. Who had a phone with a cord anymore? Only her parents' retirement house.

"Good morning."

"Don't be mad at me," Bryan's voice purred over the line. Jessica sat straight up in the bed as the night before flashed across her memory. This man had wasted her time on dates designed to get her to spread her thighs and nothing more. Her temper rose to a boil as he made a few smooching noises over the phone line as if he actually believed she'd consider them some kind of affectionate sound.

"Bryan, I'm not mad. In fact, I appreciate you bringing your lack of emotional depth in our relationship to my attention. Have a good life but I'm looking for more."

She hung the phone up with a soft hand. Her temper bled away as Jessica considered the matter finished. It was closed and sealed. The phone buzzed again and Jessica slid the thing into silent mode. A quick punch on the answering machine turned it off too. Bryan would be the one to get the message.

Slipping out of bed, Jessica hurried into her clothes. With a house full of men, it might not have been the wisest idea to sleep in the nude. Not that it mattered. At twenty-eight, she was well past the age of innocence or any kind of self-confidence issue with her body.

The morning was brisk. Jessica moved off in search of something hot to drink. The house was silent. Listening carefully for any sign of company, she walked on sock-clad feet towards the kitchen. It was very possible that her brother had moved his...friends last night.

Jessica felt a frown turn her lips down. She hadn't seen Cole in almost three months. It would have been nice to at least have breakfast with her brother.

The kitchen was as silent as the rest of the house. Sticking a mug of water into the microwave, Jessica listened to the hum it made as it heated the water. She pulled a box of tea bags from the cupboard and reached for the door of the microwave as it chimed.

With tea in hand she turned to catch a view of the morning. Her eyes fell onto her purse and she froze. She'd left the purse in the car. Looking at the black handbag with a suspicious eye, Jessica finally reached for it. Her brother didn't leave details lying around. He must have brought it up last night to prevent her from needing to cross the living room before he was ready for her to do that.

Her cell phone began singing a second later. Putting her tea aside, Jessica jabbed the talk button.

"Yes?"

"How come you're being so childish?" Bryan wasn't purring any longer. Instead his rich voice was condescending. "You said you wanted to lose your virginity under the right circumstances. I was being creative."

Jessica rubbed her forehead as she chewed on her lip. "Bryan, the right time to lose my virginity would have been on my wedding night." Even engagement night would have served but the idea of bargaining with Bryan made her feel cheep.

"You're joking, right?"

"No."

Bryan cussed on the other end of the phone making Jessica frown deeper.

"You prude! You've done everything but let me screw you. Is it any wonder I invited Gwen over? A guy's got needs and I sure as hell don't need to be shackled to any bitch just to get laid! No piece of pussy is worth that."

This time the line went dead as Bryan hung up on her. Jessica tossed it onto the table next to her purse. It didn't matter. She wouldn't let it tear her up. It was over. Sure it hurt, but Bryan wasn't worth a broken heart. He'd make Gwen a great boyfriend as long as the girl didn't want anything more. Jessica forced a smile onto her lips. All she needed was a plan.

She would just go out and beat the bushes until she found a man who wanted the whole thing—hot sex and passionate love.

"If a man isn't wise enough to understand the value of your purity, his heart isn't worthy of your affection, *darmasha.*"

Jessica didn't jump. Instead her entire body drew into a tense knot. Every muscle froze as she lifted her eyes to the doorway. She felt so horribly exposed under those black eyes. The way they moved over her body felt so intense, it was like he was touching her with the powerful stare.

Dylan stepped into the small kitchen. The female didn't move, instead she lifted her chin and stared him straight in the face. She held remarkable courage. He caught her scent on the morning air and it sent his blood racing towards his staff. This time it was an immediate reaction that needed no explanation or investigation from him. Despite her humanity, his body was demanding he claim her.

Dylan let his eyes slip over her. She was rich with curves and he found it delightful. Her breasts would actually fill his hands with their weight. Her hair was some shade between red and brown and she had it held back in a braid that only reached to her middle back. Once she was his, he'd forbid her to ever cut that beautiful mane again.

Jessica Somerton was every inch the modern woman. She had a good job, paid her own mortgage and could stare down any other technical writer in her office.

So what if she was a virgin? It was her body and her choice. Dylan's black eyes were lit with admiration. He let those sharp probes slip down her body with the slowness of molasses. When he got back to her face, Jessica felt her cheeks burning under the scrutiny.

His lips curled back into a smile. There was nothing friendly about the expression. It was pure arrogance. Jessica crossed her arms over her chest as a need to shield herself crossed her mind. It was really rather annoying the way Dylan made her emotions jump.

"Do not be frightened."

"I'm not."

She wasn't and Jessica ordered herself to believe that. Nervous and frightened were two vastly different things.

"Ahh…then your body is trembling from arousal?"

"What?" He'd stepped closer with his words, making her shift backwards. The countertop hit her back, making her face his rather overpowering body.

"Your limbs quiver, while that garment you wear displays the hardened shape of your nipples. Either you are frightened or aroused."

Dylan knew it was desire that stroked her body. His own was heating with need as he caught the delicate scent of her. Her eyes flashed at him and a grin itched to break free but her emotions balanced between fear and desire, making him frown instead. It was a grave insult to his control that any female would fear him. Dylan stepped closer as he tempered his anger. This woman had not been reared to respect a warrior's code. He would have to teach her to trust his control. Gentling her was going to be his pleasure, just as soon as he claimed her.

"Your desire pleases me greatly."

"Just hold it right there, buddy."

"Dylan."

His voice was sharp with authority. Jessica felt her temper rise in the face of his demand. She eagerly grasped at her anger as she tried to dismiss the tingle racing down her spine. A corner of his mouth twitched up in response before his hand cupped her chin.

With the counter digging into her back, Jessica was trapped. But she was fascinated as well. His eyes sank into hers a second before he leaned forward to capture her mouth.

It wasn't a hard kiss. Instead he gently traced her mouth before settling his lips on top of hers. His tongue traced the seam of her lips as he encouraged them to open and allow him access.

Her blood seemed to race through her veins as he took a taste from her mouth. His kiss was deep and warm, making her groan as heat exploded in her belly. She could actually smell his body. The hard masculine scent of a male. Her breasts lifted in response as her nipples tightened even further, the sensitive nubs complaining bitterly about the fabric covering them and separating them from the warm male skin just inches from her fingertips.

Dylan suddenly pulled their mouths apart. Desire blazed from his eyes and Jessica considered climbing up onto the countertop just to escape the overwhelming strength of the emotion. His eyes inspected every millimeter of her body before a smug smile lifted his mouth.

"You tremble with desire, *darmasha,* and that pleases me greatly."

"Get away from me." Jessica made her voice even. Her body was screaming with ten different emotions but she needed space to sort the signals into logical comprehension. Her demand made him drop his lips into a frown once again.

"Your fear is insulting. I am a warrior. Warriors do not harm females."

"I am not scared of you!" But the word "warrior" made her body respond with even greater need. The walls of her passage felt so empty as she felt the smooth slide of fluid down their surface.

"Yes, you are, and that is an insult to my control, yet do I understand you mean no harm because you are ignorant."

"You've got some nerve, I'm just as smart as you are!"

Dylan considered the flush that stained her cheeks and grunted. Trust from a female was earned, not given. It was one of the greatest gifts that any warrior could receive. Dylan stepped back and watched her chest lift with a deep breath. Her eyes immediately roamed the length of his body making him grin with pleasure.

"Jessica, will you date with me?"

He hesitated over the words almost like he was speaking in a foreign language. Jessica shifted down the length of the counter as she tried to widen the gap between their bodies. His eyes watched her as he appeared to make some decision.

"You will remember that I asked you, Jessica."

"I didn't answer you."

That smug grin appeared on the man's face again. "You are retreating."

"I am not!"

His lips curled back to show her an even row of teeth. He took one step with his long legs and Jessica felt her body jump away from the threat his body seemed to pose to hers. One black eyebrow raised in response. Jessica could have strangled her emotion-laden body.

"You accept my company? Will meet with me? I would greatly enjoy getting to know you better."

"Nothing personal but I just broke up with my boyfriend and I don't think it's a good idea. Besides, my kitchen isn't exactly the spot to be asking me out."

He grunted in response. Dylan made sure the harsh sound was the only one that escaped his mouth. She objected to the location because it gave her control over him. He felt the amusement building up behind his locked jaw. He didn't intend to play courting games like the weak human males who inhabited this planet. He would close in on the female of his choice and gentle her. Dylan indulged himself in a slow look over the woman in front of him. Heat blazed across his skin as he felt his staff stiffen with intention. But he didn't have the superior position here.

The man considered her from his sharp eyes a second before he turned and left. Jessica lifted a hand to her lips and traced the tender skin. She could still feel that kiss. It had to be one of the most intimate kisses she'd ever received. Heat was still flowing through her veins as her belly tightened into a knot of tension.

It was way too early in the morning for this!

Pulling a deep breath into his lungs, Dylan savored her scent. It was warm and soft but tempered with her tight resolve. His body responded with a rush of heat that centered in his staff bringing it to hard attention.

"She is human."

"You are young, Caius. Many species are primitive to us. A female always adjusts to Alcandian life. I have touched her mind."

Dylan gave a hard nod of approval. Her rejection stung his pride. Her feminine scent was driving his blood, causing his heart to accelerate and his body to pulse. Her body was rich with the scent of her sex. He could smell the hot flow from her body and knew she was wet for him. The hard thrust of her nipples had screamed for him to disregard her words of rejection.

Humans were too primitive to recognize that the heat he had just shared with Jessica would soon turn into a binding fever. An Alcandian warrior was fortunate to feel the burn even once in his lifetime. He had been trained since the beginning of his manhood to recognize the signs. It was the reason that drove him to hunt so far from home and on such an uncivilized world.

"It is time to return home."

"And your female?"

Dylan looked at his young training charge. Caius had completed his warrior training but needed practical experience to teach the younger man the true art of being a full warrior. "I must speak with my companion first. We must both agree to the claiming. Yet there is no doubt in my mind. Humans

23

cannot yet travel beyond their own planet. My mate will be here when I send for her."

Caius nodded agreement. Dylan forced his body to turn away from his chosen female. His hunt had been successful, but he was forced to leave her behind, and his body bitterly rebelled at that idea. Three long nights would have to pass before he could have her delivered into his keeping.

That wasn't a warrior's method. It chaffed at his pride to have to respect the laws of her planet. On his world, the clear ability to bridge with her mind was the only proof needed to claim her. It was too bad her brother had interrupted the moment of bridging. A few more moments of contact would have helped to convince Jessica of their link.

Humans weren't nearly as practical. They were too primitive to understand a warrior's need to find his binding mate. That need had driven him to five different planets as his companion-in-arms searched as well.

Dylan considered the primitive house as he signaled his home world for a gate to be opened that would allow him to return home. The smoke from the fire made him frown—he needed to get his binding mate away from the primate heat source before the toxic fumes damaged her lungs.

Light split the room as his gate opened. Dylan stepped into it without a trace of hesitation. His world had provided Earth with portals but the humans didn't hold the technology that would allow them to summon a gate anytime they chose.

Earth held only one thing that interested him. Just as soon as he found Jett, his companion-at-arms, he would make certain to remove their mate from the primitive civilization.

But it would take time and therefore patience from him.

A warrior never gave up the advantage. The gate dissipated as he stepped onto his own world. An anxious man waited for him. His companion-at-arms stood waiting as Dylan moved away from the gate portal.

"Brother, I have good news." Dylan clasped forearms with Jett before the other warrior released his stern control over his face and grinned at him.

Mind bridging was the most intimate of skills. One an Alcandian warrior only shared with his closest companion-in-arms. He and Jett had discovered the bond as youths and it had been tempered in the years and battles that had passed since then. They were closer than siblings that only carried the bond of blood. Instead their minds were linked making them more powerful when they went into battle.

Dylan relaxed his guard as Jett sought his first glimpse of the female he'd discovered. Every second of their encounter crossed to the other man as did the burning heat that had captured Dylan in her presence.

"She is human."

Jett grinned as he eyed Caius. The youth grumbled and stiffened his shoulders. A deep laugh rumbled out of Jett. The sound died away as his body jerked with a response. He could feel her through Dylan and his instincts began to surge with a need to claim her.

Dylan watched Jett closely. He knew what he felt but the signs crossing his brother's face confirmed exactly what his own body demanded he do.

She was the one. Their one mate.

* * * * *

Monday morning wasn't kind. Jessica grumbled through traffic. There wasn't enough coffee on the planet to compensate for southern California's traffic. She punched at the buttons on her radio because the morning disc jockey was running his jaw.

"Music." Issuing commands to her radio didn't get her very far. She settled for slipping a compact disc into the thing.

No one else at the office seemed in a much better mood. Yup, it was Monday all right. Time to hit the ground running.

A sharp rap on her office door interrupted her first sip of coffee. Her mug landed on her desk a second later. Her boss pushed her door open without waiting for her to invite him in and stood there with his chubby cheeks alight with excitement.

"We got the Diberman contract?"

Rodney Heithman looked confused for a moment before he shoved the door closed and scurried over to sit in front of her desk. He propped his elbows in the middle of her desk and leaned towards Jessica. She leaned closer because her boss was in the mood to share something...confidential.

"Ten times better than Diberman."

Jessica whistled under her breath. That was going to be one tall comment to back up. A contract that size just might give her the ability to telecommute. If she had only one client... "So? Spill the goods."

Her boss smiled like a cat eyeing a plump canary. "Defense Department."

They were almost holy words—at least in the field of technical writing. Getting in with the Defense Department meant living high on the hog. Once a firm made it past the rigid screening processes there would be tons of work.

"When do we start?" Jessica would sleep at her desk until the applications were finished. "I want that contract, Rodney. Me. I'm the best you've got and you know it."

Her boss's head bobbed up and down as his smile showed off his slightly crooked teeth.

"I'm talking to you, aren't I?" He pushed an envelope across the desk. "You've got an appointment today. But it's top secret."

Her boss couldn't sit still. He jumped out of the chair and winked at her as he hurried out of the room. Jessica eyed the envelope with a critical eye. It took months to get an interview. She unfolded the letter to scan it with the same critical eye.

Jessica wrote documents for a living, and this letter was top-notch. It was sharp and smooth, right down to the last detail. Even the paper was heavy grade. It was the kind of opportunity that she'd been busting her back to get a shot at. When the Defense Department wanted a technical writer, they had their choice. Her co-workers would sit up and beg for a chance at this contract.

Jessica folded the letter and tucked it into her purse. She wasn't planning on begging, but she was going to show up for that interview ready to knock them dead. Punching her computer back into its night mode, Jessica grabbed her purse and headed for the door.

She needed a much better suit.

Getting home took exactly half the time it had taken to get to her office. But instead of grinding her teeth with temper, Jessica grinned. Her dreams just might be within reach. She'd been slaving away over other contracts just waiting for one like this to come along. This was one interview Jessica intended to ace!

# Chapter Two

ഇ

"Your orders?"

"My what?"

With rigid military formality, the marine on duty extended his gloved hand again. "This is a secured location. Do you have orders to be here, ma'am?"

"Oh...um...yes I do." Jessica pulled the envelope from her purse and plucked the letter out. The marine snatched it the second the paper touched his hand. His eyes moved over it with lightning-quick efficiency before he handed it back to her.

"Identification, ma'am."

"All right." Jessica handed her driver's license over and watched the marine compare the photo with her face. He slid the card through a slot on his computer terminal before handing it back to her. She knew there was a magnetic strip on the back of all licenses now but the way this marine used it just struck her as very serious. Secured location wasn't a joke—the guy wanted to know who was on their property and they wanted more than just her name.

"Proceed forward. Do not deviate from the blue-lined areas."

The sentry stepped back and the gates opened. Jessica inched her car forward. She cast wide eyes over the armed men standing watch. Whoever she was meeting, they didn't get many surprise callers.

At least not live ones.

The road in front of her was bordered on each side by two-foot wide, bright blue painted lines. Guess that meant she wouldn't have a problem staying on the right road. The blue borders took her over half a mile through the base. Nothing looked very special. With all the security, Jessica just expected…well…something top-secret looking.

She ended up in a parking lot. The building in front of it was really very nice. It was definitely new. So far she'd only passed older concrete structures, but this was a flowing piece of architecture.

There was another set of armed guards just inside the door. This time they wanted a lot more than just her orders and driver's license — social security card, her work identification badge, even her right thumbprint were logged into a computer terminal. Jessica stared at the electronic eye that she was instructed to place her thumb in. It looked just like the one at the Department of Motor Vehicles, so she shrugged and pressed her thumb onto the lit pad.

Besides, she didn't have any skeletons in the closet, at least not any that the government might care about.

"This way, Ms. Somerton."

The hallway was pristine, with mirror-clean white tile covering the floor. The marine in front of her led her into an office that was just as spotless. A single desk sat in the center, with one chair behind it and one in front of it. There was absolutely nothing else in the room. Light came from the ceiling.

"Please have a seat."

The words were clipped and short. Jessica cast a frown at the solider but the door was closing behind him.

"Good afternoon, Ms. Somerton."

There was a second door on the opposite side of the room. Jessica flipped around to stare at the man who'd joined her. She stepped forward with a hand extended as she forced her best business smile onto her protesting lips. He grinned at her hand but sat down behind his desk without shaking it.

He was an older man with a head of gray hair. Not that he had much hair — it was clipped incredibly short. He raised his brown eyes and gave her a bright smile. Jessica felt her face fade. Everyone else at the military facility had been strictly rigid. That smile sent a chill racing towards her toes. The caring expression was out of place amidst the stanch military atmosphere.

"Ms. Somerton, have you ever given any thought to serving your country?"

"No, not really." The man's smile grew brighter, and he didn't offer his name either. Jessica fought the urge to squirm in her seat. Something felt really strange.

"I'm in a position to offer you a chance to become a true citizen of the global community." He stopped to smile at her again. "Your unique talents have been requested by one of our affiliates. But you would have to be inducted into the ranks."

"I am not a freelance agent."

"This has nothing to do with your employer."

Jessica clamped her jaw together. Questions were trying to fall out of her mouth while that chill ran down her spine again. She had that letter memorized and the words filtered across her brain where it set off an alarm. This was not the interview she had thought she'd be attending. Curiosity clamored for her to stay and find out what her host's little hints about a global community meant, but her common sense demanded she stop before reaching the point of knowing *too* much.

"You've got the wrong woman."

Jessica pushed out of her chair and turned towards the door in a fluid movement.

The door opened before she got close enough to touch it. Two soldiers stepped into the room and firmly pushed it back closed. They both flattened their backs to the wall and stood with their legs shoulder-width apart and their hands tucked behind their backs. They never looked at her.

"Sit down."

Jessica turned to look at her host, blinking her eyes as she took in the hard face. The smile was gone. The transformation made her shift between the men. She certainly wasn't going to sit back down in that chair, but another look at the door told her she didn't need to force any kind of confrontation. The wide chests of these men said she would end up the loser in any test of brute strength. That left her with her brain and Jessica certainly wasn't slow on the uptake.

"Sit down."

"No." Jessica crossed her arms across her chest instead. A smile appeared on his face again. It made her heart rate triple. It wasn't the bright one he'd been wearing. Instead, it was a cold twist of his lips.

"Your brother's career might look a whole lot brighter if you took a moment to listen to my proposition."

*Cole? Oh hell!* These looked like the kind of weird, cloak-and-dagger people that her brother ran with.

"Does my brother know I'm here?" Jessica would do a lot for Cole. Even deal with this...whatever *this* was.

"I doubt he'd object." He clamped his jaw shut and looked directly at the chair. Jessica dropped into it out of family loyalty. Alarm was racing up along every nerve in her body. If sitting in the chair would expedite matters, so be it.

"Your brother is an excellent member of our community. We're requesting you join the team."

Jessica tipped her head to look at the two sentries standing by the door. Twisting her lips into a sarcastic smile she batted her eyelashes at her host. "Request? What a tame little word."

"Your brother —"

"Can it!" Jessica leaned across the desk and slapped her hands on top of it. "I very much doubt Cole has any clue that I'm here. What do you want?"

Her host wasn't a man used to dealing with demands. Anger twisted his face. Jessica glared right back at him. She didn't like being scared, and letting her temper loose felt much more stable.

"This information is classified." Her host wasn't angry anymore. His eyes seemed to drill into her with his seriousness. "Make no mistake, Ms. Somerton, if you repeat a single word of this to anyone, you will be shot."

Abruptly, her host stood up. His eyes fixed on the two sentries. The men stepped forward in response. "Do you understand me, Ms. Somerton?"

Jessica pushed herself to her feet. The two sentries stepped up beside her. She felt trapped between the men. "You made yourself clear."

"Good." Her host turned and jerked the door behind the desk open. "Follow me."

He stepped through the doorway. Jessica hesitated, but a hand settled firmly on her arm as the two men behind her, along with their rifles, ensured any thoughts of declining never entered her head.

The doorway led to another hallway. Her heels clicked on the tiles as she quickened her steps to keep herself between the men. The grip on her arm released the second she picked up her pace.

At the end of the hallway stood a row of black glass doors, in front of which stood more guards. These sent a slight shiver down her body. Semiautomatic rifles were aimed directly at them as they approached the doors. The eyes of these sentries were sharp as their fingers rested on the triggers of the deadly weapons.

Her host pressed his palm to a black pad in the center of one of the doors. Red light outlined each of his fingers before the entire pad turned green. He turned to the guards closest to the black door and executed a sharp salute.

"I'm transporting one package."

The guard turned his eyes onto her before he returned the salute.

"Clear for one package."

Two of the guards tipped their rifles up. They used the shoulder straps on the weapons to keep them steady with only one hand on the triggers. Their boots hit the tile with hard impact as they stepped forward. Jessica was suddenly held by each of her upper arms. They pulled her forward as her host opened one of the black doors.

"I can walk just fine." Their grips tightened. Jessica sucked her breath in as pressure bordered on pain. The amount of strength in their hands was amazing. She was almost tempted to see if they could carry her along without any help from her own feet.

The second they crossed through the doors, she forgot about the grip on her body. Electric blue light illuminated the room. In front of her was a vast building, completely empty except for what looked like an airport security checkpoint. There were several men at the terminals all speaking in low tones.

Beyond them was an area the size of a football field. The corners were pitch-black, but the center was split down the length by a glowing current of electricity. It had to be fifteen feet high and it crackled like live energy. The thing glowed blue and white as it shimmered. An electric whine filled the room.

"That's a wormhole, Ms. Somerton."

"I thought they were only theory."

Her host stepped into her view. His face was deadly serious.

"And that's the way it's going to remain for the civilian population."

Jessica nodded her head. No one was playing games here. These people wouldn't think twice about shooting her if she even thought about revealing something.

"Fine. I see nothing. Now, tell your dogs to let me go."

That small twist appeared on the man's face before he nodded sharply at the guards.

"You're Somerton's blood, all right. I recognize the hellfire burning in those eyes."

Jessica rolled her shoulders as she resisted the urge to rub her arms. She'd be sporting bruises tomorrow, but somehow the idea of showing even the tiniest hint of weakness bothered her. She looked back at the pulsing current. It seemed to pulse with movement.

"Don't look directly into it. Causes eye damage."

"All right, it's time to toss me another clue." Jessica returned her eyes to her host. Wormholes were gates or tunnels to other points in the universe. Suddenly, the idea of a package being transported made her question exactly what package her escort had been talking about. The man wasn't carrying anything...except her. Looking back at the current of blue energy Jessica decided being called the package was a very disturbing idea.

"What is on the other side of that thing?"

"A planet. Its atmosphere is similar to our own. Ms. Somerton, you've been requested to serve as an emissary."

"Whoa!" Jessica stepped back and bumped into her escort. "Wormholes didn't appear in my reality as anything more than science fiction until two minutes ago. I don't think I'm interested in testing out theories or being your package."

"No?" His lips lifted into that smile again. "Not even wondering if there really is a planet on the other side of that vortex? Not curious to discover what information the government is really hiding about aliens and visitors to Earth? Don't you want to know what really goes on at Area 51?"

Jessica's eyes were drawn to the energy current once again. Curiosity raced through her brain almost as fast as uncertainty. Her thoughts were twisting together inside her head as she tried to grasp the idea of actually stepping off

Earth. Whoever her host was, he was good. He knew exactly how to lay down a trail that she wanted follow.

"Wait a second... Just who requested me? Cole?"

Jessica stepped forward. She'd suspected her brother was living in a different world. But she certainly hadn't considered that it was actually another planet. But if Cole was over there, that changed things...a lot.

"No. The Alcandians make the choices on emissaries."

Jessica's face settled into a frown once again. She moved forward to look at the terminals in front of the vortex. Twenty or so men were engrossed with computer screens. They had headsets on with slim microphones that wrapped around their jaws. Work was being carried out in a steady and very precise manner. No one paid her the slightest attention.

"Why would an...alien know me?"

Her host laid a palm in the center of her back and pushed her forward. Jessica took slow steps as her eyes moved over the terminals and the work being done. It reminded her of a surgery room. Everyone seemed focused on one collective goal.

"The Alcandians you met recently were important ones."

Jessica's eyes flew to his face. Her host looked at her with a rather firm resolution that didn't make a whole lot of sense. Well, not much in the place made sense. But there were too many facts present for her to consider it absurd.

But that didn't mean this thing was really a wormhole.

A sharp alarm blared across the room. The work pace doubled as fingers punched at keyboards. The blue light tripled as the vortex let out a sharp pop. Jessica couldn't tear her eyes from the thing. She blinked as her vision reacted to the high level of light. The entire current of the gate jumped and then went back to it original condition.

Men stood in front of the vortex. Jessica felt her jaw drop open. One second, a pop, and they were standing there. They walked forward on strong legs. The three-quarter-length coats were slit up the sides, the panels flowing with their legs.

"Oh, sweet Jesus." Jessica muttered the words under her breath. It was also a prayer, because her memory was really good. The three-quarter-length jackets and the huge muscular shoulders were way too familiar.

Was she being shut up? Jessica suddenly felt like there were hands gripping her throat. Each breath seemed to take great amounts of effort to get into her lungs. There were eight of the huge men bearing down on her. With the two guards behind her, she was trapped. Everything ran together inside her head as she tried to fend off panic.

"Where's my brother?" Her voice was edged with panic, but Jessica didn't care. She didn't have the time to figure out how to deal with these…people. Her brother had experience.

"He's on assignment."

Jessica watched the men approaching with wide eyes. They were too strong. It came from more than their bodies. She was aware of their presence in every cell of her body. They all had their eyes trained on her with a devotion that scared her right down to her toes.

Jessica jerked her eyes off the group bearing down on her. The cold smile was back on her host's face as his eyes watched her every move. Her temper exploded. She did nothing to keep the flash of temper contained. It burned away her fear, letting her catch hold of her composure.

"You are lying to me."

The smile faded as the group of aliens reached them. Jessica lifted her eyes to stare into their rough faces. The level of fitness was amazing. Their arms were held away from their bodies because of the thick biceps. All of them sported shoulder-length hair that was pulled away from their eyes with a single thin braid. Just at the front. Some had that braid hanging straight down the back of their head and others let it rest behind their right ear.

"Who speaks deception, *darmasha?*"

The man expected her to answer him. He hooked his hands through the slits in the side of his jacket and into the waistband of his pants. His eyes drilled into hers, waiting for an answer. Jessica turned her attention to her host.

"Aren't you?"

He smiled at her smugly, with a look of triumph. "If you want to know, you'll just have to test out those wormhole theories."

"I was thinking of going back home and the sweet bliss of ignorance."

The man in front of her unhooked his hands with amazing speed. One hand landed flat on her host chest's making him stumble back.

"I am Jett, duty-bound to escort you, *darmasha.*" His eyes were the most piercing things Jessica had ever seen. She could actually feel him inside her head. It was a weird feeling of having her most private emotions on display. But stranger still, was the fact that she was aware of his emotions as well. He was uneasy with her. Almost like an animal that he wanted to approach with caution because he wasn't sure if it was tame or not.

But he burst inside her head like an intimate friend, and her body responded with a surge of heat that astonished her. Jessica actually felt her breasts swell and lift for him. His eyes watched her face as his hand lifted to stroke the surface of her cheek. The single touch burned as her body responded with another wave of heat. It flowed down her body until her belly tightened and sent out a deep awareness of his large male body. She was keenly aware of just him and of his strength and ability to surround her with it.

Jett had to call up all his years of training. He wanted to touch her. Her delicate female scent drifted to his nose making the blood surge through his veins. Heat bubbled up in his chest as he watched her eyes blink and shift as she felt the current as well. The men surrounding them became his greatest concern. He had to remove her from this planet before she became unwilling to do so. Once home he would see to her worries. Females always settled into Alcandian life but they often panicked at the idea of mind bridging. Jett shut the link between their thoughts before she became any further aware of it. Her eyes blinked at the change as she considered him with suspicious eyes.

Jessica stepped back. Jett's eyes were a little too intense. They reminded her of Dylan in some deep part of her brain. He reacted immediately to her movement. He stepped beside her while his left arm opened to extend an invitation towards the gate. His right one raised ever so slightly up behind her, making the offer her only option.

"You will find Alcandar quite stunning."

"I can hope so." Jessica stepped forward and Jett mirrored her movement to not allow any more distance between their bodies. Raising her eyebrow, she looked at the huge man and his determination to hover over her. "Your invitation skills need a little work."

She felt more like a sheep being herded than an ambassador with her escort.

Jessica felt the waves of energy raise her hair as they approached the wormhole. She clamped her lips shut to contain her rapidly increasing breath. Excitement battled against her alarm at the idea of stepping off her native planet. Adrenaline surged through her bloodstream as she looked at the twisting current of the intergalactic gateway.

"I will enjoy having you explain your preferred customs of introduction and then I will tell you mine. Will you allow my escort, *darmasha*?"

Jessica jerked her face around to see if the guy was teasing her. Instead, she watched as he extended his left arm out, palm up. He waited while she looked at the hand and back to his face.

"I don't know what you mean. Aren't you escorting me now?"

He gave a slow nod of his head and moved his palm closer to her body.

"If you place your hand on top of mine, I will anchor you as we cross. The vortex is turbulent and your body is slight." His eyes dropped down her length as he spoke. She flushed under the scrutiny and felt that heat creep across her cheeks.

Jessica looked into the pulsing center of the wormhole. Casting a glance over her shoulder, she caught sight of the guards and their rifles. The muzzles of the black weapons were raised towards her.

"Some choice."

Jessica laid her hand into Jett's offered one. Forward seemed to be her only option. Jett curled his hands around her as his right arm closed around her waist. The group stepped forward and took her with them. She was going to kill her brother the next time she laid eyes on him.

A second later, the gate surrounded them with strong currents of energy that flowed around her body like a river. It pummeled against her, tossing her body like a stick in a stream. Jett's body was the only solid thing and she pressed back against him out of pure instinct.

A loud pop hit her ears and suddenly her feet were standing on firm ground again. The blue glow came from behind her now, but her vision sparkled with huge flashes of light, refusing to show her what lay in front of her.

Jett released her instantly. He stepped back that half step as his left arm issued an invitation to move forward.

Her vision returned to show her an equally large room. Yet these walls were smooth reddish-brown stone, a color that was definitely an improvement over the black glass. The group kept walking up a ramp and past another set of terminals, but there wasn't frantic movement here and there were no keyboards at these terminals. The workstations weren't manned either. The screens seemed to be automated somehow and were carrying on their work without the need for any Alcandian assistance.

A row of doors stood in front of them. The guards all turned curious eyes on her as the doors shimmered and dissipated. Jessica missed a step as she blinked but the row of doors was simply gone. In front of her was a huge courtyard built of more reddish-brown stone. Green vines trailed down large pillars bathed in afternoon sunlight.

The courtyard was packed with men. Every last one of them bound with muscle. Hundreds of eyes stared at her as she stepped into the sunlight. The hum of low conversation was coupled with numerous nods as they considered her. While it was bright, the air was chilly. Her suit was made of linen, and the lightweight fabric appeared to be an extremely poor choice to wear for intergalactic interviews.

Jessica suddenly stopped dead in her tracks. Jett bumped into her. The huge man sucked his breath in as he practically leapt away from her. Jessica stared at the opposite end of the courtyard where a man very purposely stood waiting for her.

She could see it in the hard stance of his body but the thing that made her freeze was the overwhelming sense of him. Dylan was sweeping through her brain, recalling every feeling she'd had during their brief time together.

Dylan's eyes were just as precise as the night she'd met him. He gave her exactly ten seconds before he began striding towards her. She must have forgotten how big he was because his body seemed to grow with each step he took. Jessica felt her eyes growing wide. She pushed herself forward. Now was a really bad time to try acting like a rabbit. Cole knew these people. Well, that meant she could adapt as well.

Dylan stopped to wait—watching her come to him was immensely satisfying. He used iron control to keep his face clear from expression. The afternoon wind carried her scent to his nostrils, teasing him with small traces of her essence. Temptation urged him to look over her curves again but he held her eyes instead.

He could feel the near panic coursing across her emotions. Being human, she didn't know how to shield her mind from his. That suited him rather well. Right now, it only served to build more confidence in his decision. Jessica Somerton was looking fear straight in the face with her shoulders squared. Heat began to burn in his body as Dylan considered binding her body to his.

Jessica stopped just feet in front of Dylan. His head gave the slightest of nods, but his black eyes seemed filled with triumph. She raised her chin further. Her escort all stopped and swung their right fist up to their left shoulder. Dylan returned the salute as Jett angled his head about to catch her eyes.

"Welcome, *darmasha*. It has been my honor to serve you."

A warm hand cupped her chin to bring it back to Dylan's probing eyes. He stepped towards her body until she felt his heat. He took a deep breath as his eyes narrowed to slits. The blue light flashed across the black orbs before he let his mouth curl back in a grin.

"Welcome to my home, Jessica."

Her body chose that moment to respond to his with another round of blazing heat. The walls of her passage suddenly felt hot and empty. It was such an extreme reaction that she shifted as she felt her body growing moist.

Two pairs of dark eyes watched her intently as she struggled with the extreme sexual responses. The courtyard was full of men, yet her thoughts were centered on Dylan and Jett. She barely knew them but the two warriors seemed to draw from her body a reaction that was transforming into primitive need.

The wind was picking up and she shivered. Jessica convinced herself that her reaction was to the weather. No man had ever made her tremble, and today wasn't going to be the first time for such a feminine reaction either.

Dylan frowned deeply as those sharp eyes watched her with amazing thoroughness. He laid his hand along the column of her throat and Jessica gasped. His skin was wonderfully warm again her chilled neck.

"You are dressed foolishly for this season."

"Someone forgot to tell me I'd be taking a trip today."

"I did not forget. You refused to be my date."

"You went to all this trouble to get a date that I turned down?"

His eyes narrowed in response. A strong hand curled around her arm as Dylan turned her arm and settled it into the nook of his, but his opposite hand stayed firmly settled on top of hers, making certain she was bound to his side. His legs were much longer than hers, and Jessica found herself tripling her stride to keep up with his pace. Her fashionable black heels didn't take to the event well and she stumbled and struggled to keep her balance. Dylan muttered something under his breath before he scooped her off her feet.

"Hey!" Jessica landed against his chest. His arms tightened around her when she tried to push away from the wide expanse of muscle. She squealed when Jett's face appeared in front of her. The warrior smiled at her as his dark eyes took the moment to look right up her skirt. She clamped her thighs together and smothered a gasp as the sensitive opening of her body registered the pressure as almost painful. The folds covering her sex felt swollen and too sensitive to be clamped shut by her thighs.

"You did not prefer to have our introduction on your world. So we shall have it on mine."

"I *prefer* to go home, buddy."

A set of stone stairs rose up in front of them. Dylan curled his lips back into a smile before he climbed them in a steady pace and stepped into a house of some kind.

The bottom floor was huge. There wasn't a single wall. Large columns rose up twelve feet from the walls away from the outer walls in a perfect square. They supported a second story that was open in the center. The ceiling was a huge breathtaking dome made of sparkling glass.

"This is your home." His words were soft. So soft Jessica could almost ignore them. Instead, she felt that horrible fear rising up inside her again. She hated the weakness but seemed unable to rally her temper to fight it. A huge hand gently smoothed her back in response. Her eyes flew back to Dylan to find him inspecting her face.

"You will understand in time."

"Put me down and you can explain it right here."

He raised an eyebrow instead. A second later he turned and found a staircase. Looking past his shoulder, she watched as Jett followed them, but the rest of the warriors filtered across the lower floor. The second floor was like a veranda that went around the entire building. A huge curtain was pulled back to allow them into one long side of the veranda to what was clearly a bedroom. There were chests, large chairs, and more area rugs. What looked like a fireplace was set into the wall. The bed—round with no headboard of any kind—sat in the very center of the room. Instead pillows were arranged in the center of the padded surface and the bed cover fell over its edges all the way around like a table skirt.

Dylan swept those pillows away with her body. He laid her carefully on the bed and planted both his palms on either side of her head. He lowered his body until he was a bare inch from her and deeply sniffed at her chest. His eyelids lifted to reveal another blue flash.

Heat rose up inside her. Jessica was frozen on the bed, too afraid to move and attract any more of his attention. His body was impossibly large. Every time he smelled her she trembled with arousal. She felt the quiver in her belly as she caught the warm scent from his skin.

"This is unreal! Get away from me!"

"Why? Your body trembles in need of mine. We should get closer, not further apart."

Dylan struggled with his lust. The fever was burning hotter in his blood now making it difficult to resist the urge to touch her. His mind reached into hers and found her arousal. He stroked one hand over the side of her face as he opened their link and held it steady while his desire filled her head.

"Getting closer sounds wise to my ears as well." Jett pushed the curtain aside as he strode across the chamber. His eyes were hard points that probed her. An odd sense of nervousness ran across her thoughts as she watched his reaction to her position on the bed with Dylan. It felt like she was worried about what the other warrior would think.

Jett stopped just inches from the bed and let his fingers reach for her hair. He twisted some of it between his fingers and grinned at the feeling.

Dylan shifted and rose until he was sitting on the bed beside her. Jessica immediately sat up to gain some distance from the man but Jett lowered his body onto the opposite side of the bed and she ended up sitting between their wide shoulders.

"Females are rare on Alcandar. We built the gates to find mates. Your world is more practical than most—they did not insist on being conquered. Instead they have yielded those females selected."

"No way!"

"Yet you are here, *heloni*." Dylan's fingers caught her chin to hold her gaze with his as he gave her another one of those comments that sounded like a lesson. "*Heloni* means my heart's delight in Alcandian."

Jessica felt her breath escape her body in a rush. Dylan smoothed a firm hand over her breasts. It was a gentle caress that started her breasts tingling. He gently rubbed over her nipples and smiled as they rose into tight little buttons, but when she moved away from his bold hands, her back collided with Jett. The second warrior smoothed his hands down her arms as he buried his head in her hair and took a deep breath against her neck.

"I cannot wait to taste you."

Dylan cupped her chin in a warm hold as his eyes dropped to her mouth, and his thumb came up from her chin to trace the delicate surface of her lips. Tiny pulses of sensation raced down her arms, raising goose bumps. His thumb slipped down to her chin to pull her lips apart, his mouth landing on top of hers with firm demand, pushing her lips apart as he thrust his tongue forward to taste her.

Jessica moaned softly as she burst into sensation. His lips devoured hers as his tongue moved deeply into her mouth. Fire raced towards her belly as she answered the demand of his tongue with her own, hesitantly mingling with his in a dance of intimacy. She wanted to taste him too. Jessica thrust her own tongue up to find his as her lips moved with his. Her body seemed to have a mind of its own.

Two large hands cupped her breasts as one finger found a tight nipple through the fabric of her clothing. She whimpered softly but arched her back to offer her body to the touch. Dylan raised his head as she looked down to notice that the hands on her body were not his but Jett's.

"Get away from me now!"

She was alone a second later. Both men sent her surly looks but they held their arms tightly at their sides as she rolled over to the farthest edge of the bed and stood up. Her self-control seemed to be a puddle at her feet as she tried to turn her arousal off and return to the matter of getting back to Earth.

"My mother will come to help you. Tonight, we will begin our introduction." Dylan's face was cut with anger as his eyes dropped to her nipples once more. His lips thinned as he eyed the evidence of her arousal but he stood in place.

"No, we won't. I don't know what exactly you think an ambassador does but bedroom games aren't listed in the definition where I come from." Moving back another step, Jessica stretched her spine to be as tall as she possibly could as she kept one eye on Jett as well. "Obviously there is a translation error here. You see, guys, this is called kidnapping and that's a crime on my world."

One dark eyebrow rose in response. "We are not on your planet. Here on my world females aren't so naïve as to reject what their body clearly declares."

"Boy, you've got a nerve all right. Sexual attraction is extremely common between the genders in my age group. Maybe here you drag off every woman who catches your eye but in my culture we like to fall in love before there's any sort of permanent arrangement declared."

Jett lifted one hand and pointed a finger at her like a schoolteacher. "On Alcandar there is no difference. We love and lust only for our true mate."

"Oh...and am I expected to believe you two are madly in love with me after a whole ten minutes in my presence? It's called lust, boys, and I'm not young enough to jump into bed with you because of a few compliments."

Her words were sharp and they cut into both men. They both swept into her thoughts as solidly as if they were touching her. The invasion was so intimate, Jessica felt dizzy from it.

"Get away from me!"

They were insane! Criminally insane—aliens! Disgruntled male grumbles came from both men before they turned and swept the curtain aside with a violent motion of their powerful arms. She shook her head and looked around the room hoping it would melt away like some tequila-inspired dream.

Instead the chamber remained as her body began to complain about her outburst that had sent Dylan and Jett away. Tingles of pleasure ran along her skin as her body nagged her to call them back before they got out of earshot.

That was completely absurd.

But it felt too real to dismiss.

\* \* \* \* \*

Dylan stood to consider the view from the front door. His body was surging with lust, but his mind was pulsing with the need to go back into his chamber and resume touching his mate.

Jett paced in front of him, trying to contain his envy at being the one standing outside their chamber. His brother-at-arms snorted harshly as he looked at the curtain separating him from their mate. His jaw clenched with tension as he turned to pace again.

"Human. She was raised by humans." Jett muttered the words as he tried to maintain his distance from the chamber. Jessica's womanly scent floated on the air making it nearly impossible.

Dylan rolled his shoulders and took another deep breath. There was tradition to observe. He'd never really considered the rituals that surrounded binding, but tonight they were taking on new meaning. Trust wasn't something that a female just made a gift of. Seven days hadn't seemed very long until he'd tasted her. Now the lust pounding through his body promised Dylan the longest week of his adult life.

"Patience, my son."

His mother's voice was soft as she came into view. She held her arms open making him frown. Only his mother would insist on publicly embracing a grown warrior. A hurt look entered her eyes making Dylan lean over to give her the embrace.

"There, and now I will go to greet my new daughter."

"Mother, our mate-to-be is…not very receptive."

"Ahh... But I think it most fitting that you do not have an easier time than your father did. You are so very much like my stubborn mates." Lanai winked at him before she turned to cross the hallway. Her smile was pure mischief. Dylan smiled himself. Waiting might be frustrating, but taming his little Jessica would also be invigorating.

Jett grimaced as his mother appeared and held her arms wide.

"Joy, my son. You have found me another daughter at last." Paneil clasped her hands together as she turned to look at Dylan's mother. The two women laughed as they eagerly went to brush the curtain aside. Lanai cautioned Paneil to calmness before entering the chamber.

Dylan turned and grasped Jett by the shoulder.

"Come, brother, best we celebrate below floor."

"Aye, if I hear her splashing at her bathing, I am likely to become insane," Jett grumbled as he forced himself to take the stairs to the bottom level. If their mate had been raised on Tramisah, he could go to her now. Tramisah females were raised to seek out only a male that could enter their thoughts. They often covered their eyes when meeting males in order to make certain they were not misled by handsome features.

Instead Jessica was a human. That race was the most impractical in the universe. They practiced monogamy even in the face of their unbalanced gender number. Dylan handed him a drink and Jett took a swallow from it. The hard bite of the fermented brew would be his only companion tonight.

Tomorrow, he would be more than happy to introduce his mate to the reality of their union. He lifted his drink towards Dylan.

"To our union, brother."

"To the union."

# Chapter Three

🔊

"You are freezing. The water will be wonderfully warm."

Dylan's mother was just too likable. Jessica found it really hard to continue having a mental breakdown when the woman was so easy to get along with.

Besides, the woman was correct. Jessica was certain her toes were turning blue. The stone floor was transferring the chill straight into her bones. Dylan's mother lifted her hands to motion Jessica to join her and Paneil across the stone floor.

In the back of the rectangular room was a large bathing tub. It was three feet deep and round like a hot tub. Dylan's mother had somehow filled the tub with water that was sending up fluffy clouds of steam that made Jessica shiver even more.

There wasn't a visible faucet. In fact, as Jessica got close enough to look into it she saw there was no drain either. It was strange little details like those that made her tremble. The room looked rustic but there was a definite presence of advanced technology.

"There now. Let me help you with that garment."

"Does that mean you're staying here while I bathe?"

The older woman nodded her head of amazing hair. Jessica was green with envy over the mass of naturally curly locks. It was golden-blonde and hung to her waist. She was also willow-thin. Jessica clutched her double-digit-sized suit jacket together.

"Please call me Lanai." Her small hands were actually rather strong. She pulled Jessica's hands away and had the jacket unbuttoned in a second. "I'd prefer you call me Mother, but I know this will take time."

Lanai pulled the jacket down Jessica's arms, and stared at Jessica's bra with a silly smile on her lips.

"It has been so long since I saw one of those." She had the undergarment unhooked in another two seconds. Jessica's hands flew up to cover her breasts, or the most she could cover with her hands. Her breasts had a mind of their own. They'd shown up in fifth grade and grown overtime. Bra shopping was usually an all-day event that ended at the adult store, because they stocked double Ds that didn't look like something her grandmother might favor.

"Lanai, it's nothing personal, but I'm not used to bathing with company."

"I know." Lanai reached for the waistband of Jessica's skirt and popped the button free. "But it is very common here. Leaving you to your bath would not be kind of me. The introduction rituals are very exposing for humans. It's best to get used to it now. Paneil will be back shortly with some clothing for you. You will get used to Alcandian clothing very quickly, it is very comfortable and warm."

"I have no intention of getting used to anything. Dylan might be your son but the man has abducted me."

Lanai stood back and aimed her hazel eyes at Jessica. Being able to stir guilt in the younger generation must be a skill all mothers held because Lanai's no-nonsense look was making Jessica fight off the urge to squirm.

"My son has claimed you. He will publicly bind his life to you. I remember that many human males refuse to honor their mates with such pledges. They even leave their children fatherless. An Alcandian warrior is never allowed to dishonor a female so savagely here. I have never regretted binding my heart to my warriors. Did you really have something better back on Earth?"

That sounded way too logical. Lanai snapped her fingers and held her hand out for Jessica's skirt. The waistband was open and the garment was clinging to her hips.

"Besides, do you think I don't have breasts?"

Jessica twisted her lips into a crooked line as she looked at Lanai's trim waist. With a huff Jessica pulled the skirt off her body and stepped out of it. Lanai laughed as she took the skirt and folded it.

"I have often longed for more curves. Nothing I eat sticks."

"It's not all it's cracked up to be." Jessica pulled her nylons off and gave up trying to cover her body. Lanai did have a point. Breasts were breasts. But she felt her cheeks growing hot as she turned to dip her foot into the water. She'd never even showered in a girl's gym before.

The heat shot right up her frozen foot making her sigh. It was just too tempting. Jessica climbed into the tub and sank down into the water. She felt a moment of peace, a little bit of freedom from the tangled mess she seemed to have tumbled into.

Sure, he was a hunk of a man, but that didn't mean he could bring her home like a kitten. Even if Dylan had already taken to stroking her like one. Her nipples choose that moment to bead as she recalled exactly how much she'd enjoyed that touching. The man's hands were frankly amazing.

"Lanai, I am not going to play some kind of barbarian game with your son. It simply won't work. Tell him to send me home."

Lanai dumped a pitcher of water over Jessica's head in response. She added some kind of sweet-smelling soap and began washing Jessica's hair.

"But my son will not fail. He has searched for too many years for you. It's your scent that attracted him. An Alcandian warrior's senses are never wrong."

"You're joking, right?" Jessica took a soap of some sort out of Lanai's hand while she tried to make sense out of nonsense. "Dylan is basing this whole thing on how I smell?"

"And on being able to link with your mind."

The soap dropped into the water as Jessica stared at Lanai. Shock held her still as she absorbed the idea that Dylan really could...read her mind.

"He knows everything I'm thinking?"

"No. Only how you feel. It is a wonderful unity that makes binding so much deeper."

"Can everyone one here get into my head?"

Lanai held out a towel and Jessica stepped out of the water without a thought for her nudity. Having hundreds of people tapping into her head was a whole lot more horrifying than bathing with Lanai.

"No. Only your mates will be able to. Admit you have already felt them inside your thoughts. Dylan and Jett have both touched your mind. That is why you are here, there have been no mistakes."

Jessica shook her head almost violently. Things were sounding too logical. This was insane. She had to be in a hospital somewhere with a major head injury.

"Lanai, I've brought the presentation robe."

There wasn't a door to the room. Instead whoever wanted to get Lanai's attention was simply speaking through the heavy burgundy curtain.

"She's ready."

The fabric was pulled up as Paneil angled her way into the room. She had some large piece of fabric draped over her outstretched arms.

"Greetings, daughter. I have brought you the very robes I wore to my own presentation." This exotic-looking woman had almond-shaped eyes, deep honey-colored skin, and hair of deepest black. She gently laid the fabric on the bed.

Lanai took the towel out of Jessica's distracted hold. Paneil immediately ran her eyes over Jessica's nude body. She smiled widely as she looked back into Jessica's startled eyes.

"Jett will adore you, child."

"Jett?"

"Yes, I am so pleased fate has selected my son as your companion." Paneil looked at Lanai. The women shared a bright smile before Paneil reached for the fabric she'd brought with her. It unfolded to reveal a jacket very much like the one Dylan wore. Only this one was made of a shimmering purple fabric.

The two women pulled it up Jessica's arms with gentle motions. It wrapped around her and buttoned on each side. It had an empire waistline that also had cups for her breasts, but not quite enough room. The rounded neckline gave a rather full view of her breasts as they swelled out of the top.

"Tell me there's another piece to this outfit." Jessica glared at her cleavage and tried to tuck more of herself into the jacket.

Paneil handed her a pair of matching purple pants but nothing else. The fabric was ultra-thin and there didn't seem to be any underwear.

Suddenly Jessica looked at Paneil as her initial greeting came to mind.

"Why did you call me daughter? I thought Dylan was claiming me."

"Yes, and Jett is companion to Dylan."

Jessica stared at the two smiling women. "Meaning what?"

Lanai patted Jessica on the hand before she began to play with her drying hair.

Paneil clapped her hands together as she smiled so large her eyes almost disappeared. "Jett has agreed to your union and you will become my daughter as well."

"Explain that please." There was a sinking feeling in her stomach that Jessica refused to acknowledge. The moments she'd spent sandwiched between the two warriors had been mind-numbing. One of them was plenty for any girl, but there was a wicked little whisper in her head telling her to hope she might just end up back between them again.

"Alcandian unions are not monogamous, Jessica. It is both our sons that are claiming you." Lanai said it in a firm voice. The older woman wasn't interested in any argument on the subject. She lifted her chin and seemed to dare Jessica to disagree.

Jessica wanted to. But she seemed frozen in mid-thought. Her body erupted into a flame of heat so strong she almost buckled under it. Temptation urged her to rejoice right before her common sense screamed out a warning. There wouldn't be any control in a relationship with both men. They would reduce her body to a network of receptors that responded completely to their touch.

The idea was as tempting as it was terrifying.

"When hell freezes over." She choked the words out and crossed her arms over her escaping cleavage. Jessica had always made her own decisions about sex and that was the way it would be staying. Lanai's face brightened with a large smile.

"In Alcandian lore, there is no such thing as hell, daughter."

* * * * *

The room went silent the second Jessica stepped off the bottom step. There had to be three hundred men present and she could hear her soft-soled slippers move on the tile floor. Their eyes roamed over her body making her straighten her back. She absolutely refused to respond to this insanity.

There was going to be no claiming. Not by Dylan and certainly not by both Dylan and Jett.

Paneil and Lanai each held one of Jessica's hands as they pulled her across the room. The women nodded and smiled to the many offers of congratulations they were offered.

Jett stood proudly next to Dylan. Dylan's eyes were fierce as they locked with hers. Jessica tossed her chin and glared back at the man. The corners of his mouth curled up the smallest amount. Jessica felt her lips heat with the memory of how his mouth had felt against hers. Jett's eyes were boldly focused on her exposed cleavage.

The walk seemed endless. Jessica almost sagged with relief as she was offered a chair behind a large table. It was set with eating dishes. All were different shapes than she was used to but they didn't look too foreign. The plate was square and the drinking cup was round at the bottom and came up into a short tube. Dylan wrapped his fist around the round part as he raised it to the assembled crowd. She didn't understand his words but the deep timbre of his voice made her body warm and tingly. She shifted in annoyance.

Food began to arrive on huge platters. But no one carried them. Instead they appeared over the table with a rather faint popping sound. It looked like wormhole technology had a lot of practical uses. Her stomach growled as the scent of the dinner hit her nose. Breakfast had been an entire day ago and had only been a bagel.

Jett and Dylan both piled food in front of her. But when she reached for a red-looking thing, Dylan secured her hand to the table surface.

"I'm hungry."

"And I will feed you."

He lifted a piece of food and held it to her lips. Jessica hissed at him in reply. She was not going to be fed! Of all the medieval practices! No. Not a chance.

She turned her head only to find Jett holding another morsel between his fingers for her. He grasped her left hand and bound it to the tabletop.

"I am not some pet."

Jessica stared at the people in front of her. They were tearing into the food and her stomach growled again. Lanai and Paneil both lifted eating utensils to their faces. No one insisted they eat out of a hand like a dog.

Dylan's hand turned her jaw to face him. His black eyes pierced hers as they tried to bring her to heel. Her stomach chose that moment to rumble again.

"Jessica, do not be stubborn. This is simply tradition. We feed you to show we will be good providers."

"Is that why you're holding my hands down?"

"Nay. That is so you do not hit me."

"Well, we have traditions on my planet too. Men and women are partners and that means we sit at the table like equals."

Jett's thumb slipped under her wrist and began to stroke the delicate skin. Pleasure raced up her arm. He lifted her arm to apply his lips to the same spot and she shuddered with the sensation. This time it zipped along her limb and across her body until it hit her center. His dark eyes watched her face and he lifted his lips from her skin.

"Learning to be partners begins with trust, Jessica. You refused to meet us on your world, so you will now learn about us on ours. I confess to my enjoyment of your choice."

She huffed under her breath. Jett almost laughed. His staff rose to attention in the face of her valor. The fire in her eyes promised many nights of the same in their bed. Her stomach rumbled again and Jett felt his amusement vanish.

"Come, Jessica, we can debate once you have eaten."

Jett's fingers still hovered an inch in front of her mouth so Jessica kept her jaws locked. She felt foolish but tugged on her hands as she refused to open her mouth for a public feeding.

Dylan dipped a finger into one of the sauces on her food. He painted the sauce across her tightly closed lips. She jerked away but found Jett's hand turning her back to face Dylan.

Jessica felt her mouth water. The sweet taste came through her teeth making her crazy. She didn't think she had ever been so hungry in her life. Her stomach began to cramp, begging for her to forget her pride.

She sunk her teeth into her lower lip instead. Dylan grunted under his breath. His eyes snapped disapproval at her defiance. Jessica glared right back but kept her jaw tightly closed. His lips curled back suddenly as he took a huge bite of what looked like a turkey leg. His strong jaw snapped and popped as he chewed making plenty of smacking noise with his lips. He ran the tip of his tongue over his lips before he took another large bite.

"Pig..." Jett shoved a piece of food into her open mouth. He clamped his fingers over her mouth to make sure it stayed there. Jessica snorted with fury but was forced to either swallow or choke on it. The surrounding tables cheered and raised their drinks in response. Dylan and Jett both grinned.

Jessica indulged herself in a groan. Her stomach was begging for more food. Whatever it was she'd eaten had been divine. She ran her tongue around the inside of her mouth to capture every last bit.

Dylan lifted another piece of food from the table and offered it to her. Jessica shook her head. Low laughter drifted up from the surrounding tables, making her temper flash but she pressed her lips tightly together.

Dylan tossed the food into his mouth and licked his lips again. He even licked his fingers. His tongue came out to slowly run up the length of one finger and around the tip of it. Jessica felt heat pool between her legs in response. His eyes never left her face as he licked the next finger until it was clean. Her imagination was making way too much out of the action. He'd promised to taste her tonight and her nipples tightened as she watched the way he used his tongue and lips to taste.

His newly cleaned hand dropped from sight while he held her stare. His left hand that trapped her right hand to the table gently rubbed over the back of her hand. His fingers laced themselves between hers.

His opposite hand landed right on top of her sex a second later. Jessica tried to jump to her feet but Dylan held her in her seat with that hand. Her mouth flew open in a gasp and Jett shoved another piece of food into it.

Laughter drifted up to her ears again. Jessica felt the sting of tears behind her eyelids. She didn't taste the food this time. This public display of ownership made helplessness wash over her in a wave. There were a lot of things she could handle but being helpless wasn't one of them. Dylan and Jett were stronger than her and the fact that they didn't have a problem holding her down for their amusement made it impossible to accept either of them. She wouldn't live like that. It would reduce her to a possession.

Dylan frowned deeply as her emotions turned so suddenly. Hurt was pulsing from her mind. He did not understand it. Feeding a binding mate was a custom that brought awareness to the couple.

Jessica found it shameful. Abruptly, Dylan stood up. He didn't seem able to shut her feelings completely out of his mind. Their link was forming into a bridge that would connect them mentally. His body was burning with the need to touch her, soothe her but most importantly be accepted by her. It was time to remind his little mate of just how much her own body craved their union.

Jessica kept up with the man this time. The shoes on her feet really were made for walking. That was a good thing because she was forced to a near jog to keep up with Dylan. His grip on her wrist didn't hurt, but it was unbreakable. Her eyes studied the arm attached to that hand.

Her mouth went dry as her eyes traced the sharply defined muscles that coated his arm to disappear under his jacket. He truly was the image of perfection. But the thing that stood out was his ability to control all that strength. Right now he was angry. She could feel the heat of his displeasure right inside her brain.

But you couldn't tell a thing from his body. His grip was steady and firm. It never tightened to betray his temper.

Jessica followed him willingly enough. He took her right down the center of the room. She would delight in having a few moments of privacy with the man. It was time to enlighten him about the very real fact that she was going back to Earth.

He took the stairs two at a time. Jessica scrambled to keep up. She smiled rather smugly as she made the second floor without breaking Dylan's pace.

The curtain was pulled aside. Dylan spun her forward into the chamber and unhooked the rope that held the curtain. It swooshed down to give them privacy. Jessica moved away from him. Somehow, she'd forgotten how big he was. It was like the room had shrunk now that he was in it with her.

The room itself caught her attention. The pillows on the bed were now piled onto one edge of it. The golden cover that had covered the round surface was missing. What she thought looked like a fireplace was now glowing with soft green light.

It was a scene set for seduction worthy of any bridal suite. She spun on her heel to watch Dylan. His black eyes were focused on her as he crossed his arms over his chest. His face seemed to set with firm determination a second before he unhooked the fastenings on his jacket and pulled the garment off.

"What are you doing?" It was a really stupid question, but her mind was practically blank. His chest was sculpted to perfection. She wanted to run her hands over every inch of the muscles just to see how they felt, and the strength of that desire horrified her. Exactly when had lust taken up chief position in her brain? She was a logical, front brain-thinking woman.

"I am taking my clothes off." The pants went down his legs as Jessica tried to keep her jaw from dropping too. He walked towards the bed and her eyes caught a view of his naked backside. His legs were amazing and cut with powerful muscle. The idea of having a completely irresponsible sexual fling had never seemed so understandable. Jessica felt moisture gathering inside her passage as she thought about it.

"Since you do not wish to eat, it is time we learn more about each other." He rolled his frame onto the bed and stopped on his side facing her. One large hand gently patted the surface of the bed but one of his thighs had bent and covered his cock. Disappointment made her frown as she caught herself wishing she'd gotten a look at all of him. "Come here, Jessica. I am eager to learn."

Eating out of his hand was suddenly looking like a better option. Her own weakness made her angry this time. Jessica shook her head as she gathered her courage.

"I'm flattered, really. But this isn't something I'm interested in. It's nothing personal but there is no way this could work."

"I can smell the sweet flow from your body. It will be my pleasure to show you exactly how well we will work."

Jessica felt her eyes widen at the blatant sexual comment. He sniffed at the air and pulled in a deep breath that lifted his chest. He drifted inside her head again.

"Stop that!" It was too exposing. Jessica slapped her hands onto the sides of her head, trying to hold onto her private thoughts. She felt a flame of frustration from him before he pulled out of her mind.

"Truly, I do not understand you."

Dylan rolled off the bed in a fluid movement. He walked in a semicircle around her while his eyes considered her.

"Of course you don't understand me. How could you? We're complete strangers." Jessica turned to keep him in her sight. She didn't like the way her own words sounded. They actually hit her ears as sad.

"I will change that, if you give me the chance." He moved around her again. His body seemed to pulse with restlessness. She was keenly aware of how powerful he was. The walls of her passage coated with fluid that made her notice how much she wanted to just toss her thoughts aside and simply feel. Her eyes were drawn to his erection.

"Look, buddy—"

"Dylan."

Jessica jumped as he growled the word. Her temper was trying to rear its head and she was getting ready to let it have its way. She schooled her face to calmness. Using his name wasn't too much of a concession.

"All right, Dylan, I do not just go home with strangers. I want to return to my own world."

Dylan crossed his arms and grinned. It was a huge expression of amusement. Jessica considered the prime picture of maleness that he made. Her body flushed with heat and she enjoyed it for just a moment. It was an incredible rush of sensation that she'd never felt before.

"You think I am primitive." She blushed with guilt. Dylan raised an eyebrow before he raised a single finger. "We are millennia ahead of your own people. One of the advances in our technology has taught us to recognize our mates. You humans still mill about searching out each and every sexual impulse. Alcandians no longer need to act like animals in a herd. Instead we recognize the difference between mere attraction and true binding passion."

Dylan moved forward on strong steps to gently grasp her chin. He deliberately let their minds merge in a single thrust of mental linking. Jessica felt her nostrils flare slightly as she felt his desire. She actually felt it as hot and intense as her own. It was like they were each looking into a mirror and seeing themselves reflected in the other's soul.

Dylan suddenly cut the connection leaving the spot inside her mind empty.

"You see my mind has been trained to identify this reaction. Only true mates can bridge their minds together as we just did. It is unmistakable. Your human culture has not yet made the scientific discoveries that prove I am right. Yet it does not matter, your body is already reacting to mine."

He released her chin and her eyes dropped to the hard thrust of his cock. The thing stood at attention as the top of her thighs became wet. It was so intensely sexual but she just couldn't help looking at the swollen head of his erection. Her fingers itched to touch it as the curtain moved aside and Jett entered the camber. One of his hands balanced a large tray of food that had steam rising from it.

The smell of food captured her complete attention. Her stomach rumbled with appreciation.

"Will eating here please you?"

Oh God, would it. She was so hungry it hurt.

"I can feed myself?"

Jett huffed but actually considered her question.

"Why is it so important for you two to feed me?"

Dylan's eyebrows rose with comprehension. He walked back across the room to lie across the bed again. His body rested on his side with one elbow propped onto the bed to raise his head up. He looked completely at ease, but he also reminded her of a tiger. The ability to pounce was declared by his heavy muscles.

"It is a way for us to become less strange to each other. Learning to touch another must begin with simple actions. Come here, Jessica."

His words were hard with arrogance, but she had to admit that it suited him. His mind was lightly touching hers again.

His little mate perched one half of her bottom on the bed. She even kept her hands tightly twisted in her lap. Her body was as stiff as a tree, and she raised her chin with pride.

"Feed me."

"Excuse me?" Jessica looked at his face as he smiled at her.

"I am hungry. Feed me." His smile turned mocking. "Unless you prefer Jett."

The other warrior leaned against the wall. His eyes were twin flames that watched her tiniest move, but he wasn't jealous. His lips curved into a smile as she looked at him.

Jessica reached for a piece of food before she thought better of her actions. She thrust it forward but had to lean across the bed to get close enough to Dylan's face. He nipped it out of her fingers with a sharp bite. She watched longingly as he chewed it up with slow motions.

Dylan reached for the platter next and offered her a very tempting morsel of hot food. Held up to her face, she could practically taste it just from the delicious aroma. Her stomach clenched and she bit into it out of sheer temptation.

Jessica shook off her guilt. They were feeding each other. That wasn't the same as being fed like a pet from its master. She reached for another item and offered it to Dylan. He smiled a friendly grin before nipping it out of her fingers again.

The food disappeared quickly. Jessica reached for the last piece and offered it to her companion. His grin turned serious as he snaked out a hand to capture the wrist holding the food. His fingers were solid steel as they held her hand in place.

His teeth appeared to nip the food away. He swallowed it quickly and returned to touch his tongue to the tip of her finger. Jessica jerked her hand but his strength was far too great. The velvet tip of his tongue licked over one finger and then back up as he cleaned away the drops of sauces left from their meal.

His lips closed over her finger to gently suck on it. Heat seemed to travel right down from her hand, through her arm and into her body. His tongue stroked over her finger again while his lips remained around it.

Dylan carried her palm to his mouth where he drew a lazy circle in the center of it. He licked over the surface of her hand to the delicate skin on the inside of her wrist, turning her hand over to gently bite her. Her gasp hit his ears, making him grin. He rubbed his thumb over the veins in her wrist to feel the frantic pace of her heart. The tiny veins betrayed her passion.

"Let my hand go." Jessica stared in confusion as his fingers released her wrist. He was floating inside her head again, sharing his growing desire through the mind-bridge.

"Now it is your turn to touch me."

Jessica shook her head. His eyes were almost mesmerizing. The devoted attention made her giddy, made her feel like she was beauty incarnate just because his eyes worshiped her.

"If you forfeit your turn, it will be my turn to touch you again."

"I'm not forfeiting." There was no way Jessica would give him that opening. She looked over his body and tried to decide what touch might be the least personal. Her eyes were drawn to the sculpted ridges of his chest.

"This is ridiculous." Jessica pushed her body up off the bed. She didn't have to play any game. It was her body, and her choice.

She ended up facing Jett. He was so close to the bed that when she stood up she turned right into his embrace. His arms captured her as his eyes flashed above her face. His mouth captured hers a second later and she moaned with the sheer heat of the kiss. His lips moved firmly over hers as his tongue thrust deeply into her open mouth.

Her hands landed on the firm chest in front of her as she kissed him back. A second hard male body appeared at her back as Dylan joined their embrace. That voice inside her head clamored with delight as they once again placed her in the middle of their embrace.

"I will go mad if I do not touch you." Jett's voice was thick with desire as his hands smoothed down her arms.

A curl of excitement hit her belly. Jessica jerked against their hold as she frantically tried to recover her self-control. Her blood was racing through her veins at near light speed. Her lungs increased their rate to keep up and she suddenly noticed exactly how warm and male Jett's skin smelled. She held one of those breaths as she savored the pure strength contained in his scent. It surrounded her, seeping into her skin's pores, tempting her to press closer.

Jett's taste pushed her towards complete abandon. Her nipples screamed for freedom from her clothing as her fingers pulled on the fabric covering Jett's chest.

Dylan's lips grazed over her neck drawing a moan from her as Jett released her lips. His teeth gently nipped along the same path, making sharp little stinging sensations rip into her body. It was intensely pleasurable on a scale that she'd never felt. It was like discovering her skin had nerve endings. Pleasure was moving up from his lips like heat waves.

Jett removed his mouth and she whimpered at the loss. "Turn to me, *heloni.*"

Jett helped her turn in their embrace until she found Dylan's face. His eyes dropped to her lips before he bent his head to kiss her. She didn't close her mouth. Instead Jessica welcomed the thrust of his tongue. He stroked the soft surface of her tongue, gently caressing it. Her fingers rejoiced as she laid them on his bare chest.

The two buttons holding her jacket closed suddenly opened. Jessica wasn't even sure whose hands were responsible. Both men surrounded her, their hands smoothed and gently gripped, sending pleasure coursing through her like a flood. Her sex throbbed and ached for her to let them do anything they wanted with her. All her dark hour fantasies rose above her logic as pleasure flooded her brain.

"You are more beautiful than any dream."

Dylan's voice was rough with emotion. Jessica opened her eyes to see him staring at her bared breasts. His hands closed around the globes and gently lifted them. His thumbs flickered over her nipples making her body shudder with need.

Jett reached around her hip and laid a firm hand over her sex. Only the thin layer of her pants separated him from the wet flesh that ached for his touch.

Pleasure was knotting in her belly so tight it bordered on pain. His fingers gently rubbed against her most private flesh, making it pulse and twist with demand.

Her hips lifted for him as her face drew tight. Dylan watched as she shuddered and pushed up into his hand a second before he felt release slam into her, a thin cry escaping her lips.

Dylan threaded his fingers into her honey brown hair and delivered a harsh kiss to her mouth. It was a brand of ownership that demanded surrender from her. She shifted under the assault but he pushed into her mouth and kissed her deeply.

Abruptly Dylan raised his head. Jessica gasped for control. She lifted her eyes to find Dylan looking at her with hard eyes. Jett turned her head and caught her mouth with his as Dylan turned her into the other man's embrace.

Oh God. Jessica felt her face turn beet red. Had she really just climaxed in front of two men right through her pants? Her body was heavy with satisfaction, proving that she really had

found her pleasure. It had been such an intense orgasm —
unlike anything Bryan had ever managed to bring her body to.

Dylan tipped her chin up to inspect her eyes once more.
Defiance still flashed from their golden depths, but it held little
meaning with the heavy scent of her pleasure filling his senses.

It should have made her scream. Instead she felt so
cherished in that moment. She'd been desperately longing for
a man who would want a committed relationship. Now she
had two men who seemed to want to focus on her completely.
It confused her, making her itch to squirm away from their
glittering eyes. The need for space pressed against her skull.

Dylan dropped another kiss onto her mouth before he
swept her off her feet and laid her on the surface of the bed. A
smug expression of satisfaction sat on both their faces before
Dylan stood up. The two men clasped forearms before they left
on silent steps.

It was flatly impossible. Her body was still pulsing with
satisfaction making her limbs heavy. Jessica tugged a blanket
around her as the loss of Dylan's body made her chilly. Her
eyes dropped closed as she tried to force her brain to function.
Sleep refused to let her continue the battle.

Tomorrow she could make Dylan send her home...
Tomorrow she would think of a way.

# Chapter Four

## ℘

"Good morning, daughter!"

Jessica tried not to shudder. But there was something about the pure joy in both Lanai's and Paneil's voices that demanded she rebel on behalf of all non-morning people everywhere.

Neither woman noticed anyway. They were busy pulling the window curtains open. Then they moved to the wall that overlooked the lower floor. They pulled what Jessica had believed to be wall hangings and they swished aside to reveal that there was only half a wall. It was like a balcony. You could lean over and look down into the bottom floor of the building.

Men were busy eating and talking to one another. The conversation drifted up to her ears. Several men noticed her and lifted their drinking cups to her. Jessica sprang back from their view. Her face flooded with dark color. If she could hear the people below her, then that meant they had heard her and Dylan and Jett when they were... Oh damn.

"*Darmasha?* May I enter?"

Paneil clapped her hands with delight as she hurried over to the room's entrance. She pushed the curtain aside to let three women in. Their arms were each covered with fabric. They all called greetings out as they came closer.

Lanai made slight tsking sounds as she tried to unhook Jessica's pants.

"You should not have slept in these."

"Dylan and Jett must work harder to keep their *heloni* warm without her garments." A round of giggles came out of the women but Jessica stared in fascinated wonder as the bed

68

she'd slept in suddenly made itself. The rumpled sheets dissipated with another blue flash and then new ones appeared. The missing coverlet reappeared as the pillows neatly positioned in the center of the bed.

All right, there were some things about this place she was really beginning to like.

Lanai pulled Jessica's hair over her shoulder to run a brush through it. Jessica crossed her arms to cover her bare breasts. There were also a few things she didn't think she'd ever get used to.

"Come, Jessica. You must bathe as there is much to do today."

Jessica looked at the three women and back at Lanai's firm face.

"So, I'm bathing in front of everyone today?"

The giggling stopped as Paneil looked at her with worry. The other women simply looked confused. Paneil walked over to lift one of Jessica's hands. She rubbed the top of it gently.

"You are so lovely."

The woman was just too sweet. Jessica felt herself give in to guilt. She let Lanai pull the pants down her legs and Jessica stepped out of them. Paneil's smile widened as she pulled Jessica towards the bathing pool.

All five women seemed to think it necessary to help Jessica bathe. They didn't miss a single inch of her body. Jessica was caught between the need to scream or cry. But every time she avoided a sponge, Paneil would start rubbing the back of her hand.

Lanai came forward with a towel and wrapped it tightly around Jessica's head. The women made certain not a single hair escaped that towel.

"Keep your face out of the water now, Jessica. But keep your arms in the water."

"All right." It certainly wouldn't be too hard. There were half a dozen hands holding her neck and head as Paneil moved off to one side. Jessica watched as the woman pressed her hand onto what looked like one of the hundreds of stone blocks that made up the wall. Right where her hand touched, it lit up a glowing green. Paneil looked at it and quickly tapped something. There was a faint charge to the water, almost like a static electric shock.

"There. Stand up, dear."

Jessica stood up in a second. Nervousness ran down to her toes as she tried to decide if she wanted to ask what they'd done to her. The girls all dipped large pitchers into the tub and poured the water over Jessica's body.

"Sweet Jesus." Jessica sprang away to the opposite side of the tub and looked down as each and every single pubic hair she had washed away with the water. She lifted her hands to see the skin was as smooth as a baby's. Not a single hair was left.

"Relax, Jessica. It is part of the introduction rituals."

"Then it won't hurt anyone to explain things before you do them to my body!"

Jessica glared at the bright smile on Paneil's face. Everyone was looking at her like some virginal sacrifice that needed to be soothed and gentled.

"I have a perfectly sound mind."

They smiled brighter. They weren't even interested in understanding her. To their way of thinking she should just stand still and be dressed like a porcelain doll. Loneliness swept through her in a slow wave. There wasn't a single friend she could reach for any companionship. The feeling that she was completely alone made her ache.

Paneil held out a towel and Jessica stepped into its folds without really thinking. Well, she didn't need to think. Everyone seemed all too willing to take care of thinking for her. The term "brood mare" came to mind and stuck there.

The women milled about her. They primped her and fluffed her. Lanai looked over the new clothing that had come with the three women. She used a critical eye to look at the fabrics and then at Jessica before she selected one.

At least this coat fit her. Her breasts weren't trying to escape through the neckline. Jessica turned to look at her reflection — the garment fit her like it was made for her. It was really quite comfortable. The top was lined with something silky smooth and her breasts felt almost exposed as the decadent fabric cupped them.

The shoes were lined with a soft thick fur of some type and buttoned up the outside of her ankle. They reminded her of an Indian moccasin. Once again it was as if they had been cut for her foot alone.

"They did a wonderful job. I cannot wait to see her binding robes." Paneil was clapping her hands together again. Lanai gave Jessica a long sweep of her eyes before she nodded with approval.

"You look lovely, daughter."

They began to lead her out of the room again. Jessica refused to go.

"Where are we all going?"

The girls look confused but Lanai lifted her hands to silence them. "My son waits below for you. He will answer any questions you have."

Well, that made sense. After all Dylan had brought her here. A tiny blush stained her face as she nodded her head and stopped taking her temper out on the man's mother.

Dylan sliced into her mind and she shivered as her body erupted with eager excitement. Jessica shook her head and searched for him. Her face flooded with color as she caught a look at the man. He was wearing midnight blue today, and it should have been against the law for a man to look that good.

It was just the way he stood that made him look so powerful. His legs were slightly apart and his arms held away from his body. The coat didn't hide the wide chest that declared so much power. The way his eyes watched her made the heat travel down her neck and into her stomach.

Jett stood one full pace to the left of Dylan. They were stiff and formal as their mothers led her forward. A third man stood in back of them wearing another one of those bright smiles.

Jessica felt her teeth grind together. She didn't need to be coddled. All she needed was to go home and take care of herself. Hundreds of eyes were watching her as she was once again led through the center of the room, but there was something so respectful about the way they led her in front of the entire crowd. Dylan and Jett weren't trying to avoid commitment, instead they were standing proudly in place as their friends watched.

Dylan stepped forward as his mother placed Jessica's hand into his. Paneil did the same with her opposite hand and her son. The unknown man behind him stepped forward to speak.

Jessica stared at his lips as her brain seemed to drift between languages. She was thinking in English, yet understanding what this man said. Only he was speaking a language she didn't even know the name of.

The rigid tone of his voice hit her as her brain translated the words.

"Do you swear you come to this declaration free of binding to any other?"

"I swear it." Dylan's deep voice was loud enough to bounce off the walls. His mouth curled back into an arrogant grin.

"*Darmasha*, are you free to bind yourself?"

She didn't answer. Dylan squeezed her hand and she shot him a lethal look. He sunk into her head making his demand clear. Jessica refused him with every thought she had.

"Forget it. I'm not making any promises."

His eyes almost glowed. Jessica stared at the intense anger displayed but she wasn't backing down. They were trying to get her to agree to something without explaining it to her. In other words, pull the wool over her eyes.

Well, not her! No way. People signed contracts all the time without really reading them and they ended up stuck.

"It is not a promise." Dylan tipped her chin up to gain her attention. The fever was growing in his body. Touching the smooth skin of her face made his hands hungry for more of her warm skin. "It is simply a statement that you have made no promises to any others and are free to make a vow should you choose to."

Jessica tilted her head to look at the man who had asked the question of her. He nodded his head in agreement with Dylan. Jett was pegging her with a strong disapproving look from over Dylan's shoulder. The whole room was full of men who stared at her with intense eyes. The pressure pushed against her almost like a physical force but she forced herself to hold her mouth closed. Making a rash decision might land her in a marriage for all she knew.

"Jessica, have you promised yourself to another warrior?" Dylan was jealous. He felt it burn along his body. She belonged to him!

"Renounce him now or I will challenge him!"

"As will I." Jett stepped forward with a deep frown marking his face.

"Relax, boys, there isn't anyone."

Dylan turned his head to the man in front of them. He dipped his head in a rather slow nod. She was being dragged back up the aisle in Dylan's wake a second later. Jessica yanked on her arm but it had no effect on the man pulling her towards the corner stairs. His shoulders were rigid with fury. It should have frightened her to think that she was about to find herself alone with an alien that was royally ticked off with her.

But Jessica wasn't afraid of him. It was really odd, but she just had some deep instinct that told her Dylan would never physically hurt her. The curtain swooshed down behind them as Dylan spun her free. He placed his body in front of the exit.

Dylan let his eyes slip over her curves. His staff had risen to sharp attention the second she entered the hall. Now, her scent surrounded him making his blood heat. Her body didn't seem to be reacting to their bond as quickly as his was. It was time to strengthen that bond.

Jessica felt her mouth go absolutely dry. Dylan quickly shed his clothes again. She should have told him to stop but her throat had shrunk up as she watched those amazing shoulders come into sight. He reached for his pants and bent to pull them down his legs.

He stood up with amazing slowness. His legs were as powerful as his arms, every muscle clearly defined. His chest was covered in a coat of dark hair that traveled down his abdomen and right to his... Oh, Lord.

His cock stood stiffly away from his body. Suddenly Jessica felt her nipples tighten. It was almost painfully quick. Heat seemed to shoot right into her belly and she actually felt fluid easing its way down her passage.

Oh God, she was a slut. There was no other reason for her body to react so strongly. She'd seen a naked man before. Well, maybe not one like Dylan but a cock was still the same, wasn't it? Her eyes dropped to the swollen length once again as she admitted this cock was certainly nothing like Bryan's. All males were not created...equal.

"You see, Jessica. Our scientists learned long ago to separate lust and emotion in our brains. You are my binding mate. Your body is trying to tell you that. The arousal will become acute, until it is like a fever."

"That's nonsense." It had to be. Jessica looked at his stiff cock again and felt the insane urge to taste him. Slip her lips around the ruby head and see if he would groan at her command.

"What makes no sense is your determination to resist. Did I not prove it to you last night?"

He was stepping closer with a stride that reminded her of a large predatory feline. Jessica shifted away from him. "All you proved was that my body works the way it's designed to. Orgasm is a result of stimulation." And lord knew, between Dylan and Jett her body had been on the verge of combustion.

"So, you've been brought to pleasure before?"

"Yes."

"You said you were a virgin."

Jessica bit her lip. She was tempted to lie to him. Maybe he wouldn't want her if she wasn't a virgin. A wave of hurt hit her as she considered him rejecting her. Somehow, she had to get out of this without using deception. She just didn't want to let Dylan down by lying.

"I am, but I've experimented with touching."

She shifted away from him again. Dylan smiled. She was bold and he liked her that way—strong and determined to find out about life. Her passage would be tight and her mind open to playfulness.

"Take your garment off."

He said it gently but his eyes were harsh. Jessica felt a shiver run down her spine. He was arrogant with his demand but she found it incredibly arousing. Lanai had been correct about one thing—the men here didn't treat women like disposable items. Dylan was demanding her but he was also insisting on a very immediate and public relationship. The man was a warrior. Jessica considered that word as she applied it to Dylan. If ever she'd met a real live warrior, this man was it. No doubt about it.

"Jessica, why are you ashamed of your body?"

"I'm not ashamed." Dylan looked at her with doubt and Jessica propped her hands onto her hips.

"Then take the jacket off."

"I don't just get naked with anyone who asks me too."

"I am your binding mate."

His words were cut with his frustration. Dylan schooled himself to patience as he watched her chin rise up in defiance of his claim. His control was rapidly thinning. The way she was digging her heels in seemed to issue a challenge to him.

Dylan sliced into her mind. The contact was overwhelming. His desire was so thick she could barely breathe. He was searching through her head and reading her like a book. But he held his position like some kind of boundary.

"Last night Jett didn't ask me to take the jacket off, he just did it."

Dylan's eyes glittered at the memory. Her nipples beaded and begged her to uncover them. "Why is that, Dylan?"

"It is simple." Jessica turned to see Jett giving the curtain a firm tug to keep the doorway covered. "Now that we have publicly pledged our names to you, you must decide when to yield your body to us."

"No bargaining tactics, hmm?"

"Remove the garment and let me show you what a man does with his mate. I have dreamed about your nipples since last sunset."

She believed him. Pure determination sat right there on his hard face to prove it to her. Lust had never controlled her before but it was the honest truth that she'd had similar dreams. Jessica kept waiting for guilt to show up from her conscience, but it never did. Instead all she wanted was to see the look on Dylan's face when she let him see her again.

Warm fingers cradled her cheek. Jessica jumped as she looked into Dylan's piercing eyes. Her nostrils flared slightly as she caught the deep scent of his skin. She'd never noticed that men had different scents before. She took another deep breath and considered the very unique way Dylan smelled, and her memory took that instant to remind her of the powerful image that Jett created with his scent. It triggered a rush of warmth in the pit of her belly. Dylan's fingers smoothed over her face as he watched her with approving eyes.

"Stop hiding from my eyes, Jessica. You let a man that would not honor you with his name see you. Why do you refuse me?"

That was a really good question. Jessica struggled with her body's impulses, and tried to remember exactly what it was about Dylan that she objected to. Her skin was alive with tiny little pulses of feeling that were begging to be free to grow into the kind of pleasure that Dylan and Jett had showed her last night. Her body craved to be pressed between their hard forms once more where pleasure crashed against her skin like an incoming tide.

"You can't just abduct me and expect me to welcome you. I'm not an exotic intergalactic pet."

"I do not think you are a pet. Would I offer you my word if you held no value beyond the use of your body?" He snorted as anger shot out from his eyes. "Advancing our technology has strengthened our need to find only our true binding mate. A thousand years ago, we were content to lay with females that we could not bridge with. Now that my mind had touched yours, anyone else would leave me empty."

Jessica licked her dry lips. She was so hot. Dylan's words bounced around inside her brain making her feel intensely attractive. The jacket Dylan wanted her to take off was suddenly too tight around her breasts. The heat from his body intensified that heat. One of his hands stroked over her hip in a smooth motion but he didn't reach for the little button that was just a few inches up her torso.

A deep groan came from him when she licked her lips again. His eyes were alight with desire. The hand on her cheek slipped into her hair as he lowered his mouth to hers. The contact was shocking. She gasped and he took complete advantage of her open mouth. The firm thrust of his tongue invaded her mouth. The hand on the back of her head gently tipped her head back for his kiss. He nipped and licked at her lips before stabbing his tongue back into her mouth to find hers. He used the tip to stroke her and tease her into dancing with him.

"Take the jacket off, Jessica." Jett bit the smooth column of her neck making shivers race down her spine. The tip of his tongue came out to lick each bite with a warm lap. Jett never moved towards that button either. Instead he licked and nipped his way to her ear where he captured the lobe in his mouth.

Jessica gasped and let her head fall back into Jett's chest. It felt so good. Waves of need were washing over her. Her nipples were begging for freedom, to be included in his suckling. But the fact that both men refused to take what they wanted made her reach for the button herself. It had been so simple for them to capture her. Her own government seemed quite willing to assist them, but asking *her* to take that jacket off gave her back the power of choice.

She popped the button free. The jacket immediately fell open. Jett let her earlobe go and turned her head to lock his eyes with hers. "Show yourself to us." She shivered at the husky tone and shrugged her shoulders. The fabric slipped down her arms with amazing speed.

"Now the pants."

"I can't."

Dylan let his eyes drop to her breasts and Jessica felt his gaze actually touch her bare skin. He raised his eyes to her face. "Why not? I hide nothing from you. You enjoyed looking at me."

"But your body is amazing."

"My body is a weapon." Dylan released her head and lay down on the bed. The pillows went spilling to the floor behind him. He lay on his side with his head propped in his hand. His opposite hand gently patted the surface of the bed in front of him. Jett's hands smoothed over her bare sides before reaching for her breasts. He growled against her throat as his fingers curled around each mound.

"But your body is a creation of pleasure. Every curve is sculpted to accept me. You cannot understand if you do not join with us." Dylan patted the bed again as Jett's coat hit the floor next to her feet.

They were just so damn sexy. She couldn't help but stare at Dylan's swollen cock. It thrust out from his body straight at her like some kind of proof that she was attractive. Jett's erection nudged her leg as he gently pinched her nipples.

This was pathetic! Jessica pulled her little boots off before she yanked the pants off her body and tossed them across the floor. She did not have a self-confidence issue. A sexy man had invited her to get naked with him. It was a simple enough thing to deal with. Going through that wormhole must have fried her brain.

She watched Dylan's eyes drop down her length. She felt her lips lift into a small grin as his lips curled back from his teeth. His face became a mask of arrogant possession. She propped her hands onto her hips and waited for Dylan to meet her eyes.

"Now come here."

His voice was deep and almost harsh. His hand wasn't patting the bed, instead his fingers were curled into a fist that pulled at the fabric of the sheets. Jett's hands moved from her breasts and over her hips to the bare cheeks of her bottom. Need and heat combined inside her passage as she ached for one and maybe both of the hard cocks.

"I'm not making any promises."

Dylan ground his teeth together. Her eyes immediately went to the clenched muscles of his jaw. She was too close to him. It would be very easy to pull her down by a wrist. Dylan savored the idea and the pleasure it would bring him. Her nipples were large and brown. They begged to be tasted while she stood there trying to deny his claim.

Dylan grinned in spite of his raging impatience. The ride between her thighs was going to be hard and long. She wouldn't give quarter and neither would he.

He rose up off the bed in a fluid movement that proved what he'd said about his body. It was a weapon. A weapon that was honed to razor precision. He landed on his feet a foot from her body. His eyes looked anything but friendly. Instead, pure aggression seemed to pierce her.

"We have three moon risings to gain your body's surrender. When you yield your body to our possession we will exchange the first season vows."

His arm snaked around her waist, lifting her with amazing ease, just like the night they'd met. Her toes hung just below his knees as Jessica gasped with the sensation their naked bodies produced. Every nerve receptor she had must have fired off. The signals were overloading her brain, making her want to dissolve into a quivering mass of emotion.

Dylan rolled onto the bed, taking Jessica with him. His shoulder hit the surface first to cushion her fall. He rolled, coming up over her as his legs tangled with hers to keep her thighs separated.

His voice deepened to a husky whisper as he sniffed along her throat. "All you must say is no."

The pure confidence in his tone made her moan. It was a sound born from the rapid pulsing of her body. With his body pressing along hers all she want to do was touch him. Tell him no? Oh God.

Dylan nipped her neck with a sharp bite. Not quite painful but sharply intense. He lapped it with the soft length of his tongue. Jessica caught Jett as he joined them on the large bed. He eyed her breasts like a starving man as he reached for one of the bare globes.

"Your breasts are magnificent. I'm going to suck on your nipples until I smell your body heating for my staff, *renina*." Jett's eyes glittered with possession as he looked into her eyes. "*Renina* means treasured one. I will always call you that, Jessica."

He raised the breast up as his mouth dropped to its tip. Jett sucked the entire nipple into his mouth. He pulled on it with deep motions as she tried to keep her hips from jerking. It was like her nipple was connected to her belly. Liquid fire seemed to shoot straight from his sucking right into her passage.

His tongue joined the play as his hand gently squeezed her flesh. He worried the nipple with the tip of his tongue before he returned to sucking on it with lips that were strong and hot. His cock was hard against her thigh. She seemed far too aware of the thrust of it against her leg. Her brain instantly began to remind her how much she wanted to taste him…them.

Dylan stroked his fingers across her belly. She was magnificent. She quivered in his arms as he moved down her length to her newly exposed sex. He gently stroked the hairless mound before he sent a finger into the soft folds. She was wet for them. Dylan pulled the rich scent into his lungs as he pulled his finger from her and her hips lifted for another stroke. His skin glistened with her juices as he probed her passage again.

"Your body speaks with far more honesty than your lips."

"Wanting sex and wanting you are two different things."

Dylan frowned. Jessica forced herself to keep her eyes open. His finger was running up and down her sex. Sensation tightened under his touch making her push her hips towards that hand. Relief from the building tension was quickly becoming more important than anything else. He found the little nub at the top of her folds and gently rubbed its surface. Need exploded as her bottom lifted to press her body against his hand.

"It is the same thing."

"No… I need more…than just sex."

Dylan frowned deeper but she didn't see it. Instead her eyes found Jett's cock and her fingers reached for the hard flesh. A hard male gasp was her reward and the sound inspired her. She slipped her fingers down his length as she tasted the swollen head. Jessica opened her lips to get them around his cock. Jett released a harsh grunt as she slipped her fingers back down his length again. The male sound of delight completed the embrace. Her body was being tumbled by the waves of pleasure but she craved to take both men with her.

Dylan thrust a finger into her passage once more as she continued to lick her way around Jett's cock. Lying between the two men seemed to make her sex drive explode. Jessica wasn't interested in thinking. She wanted to drown in the pure excesses.

Dylan spread the lips of her sex before she felt the warm brush of his lips. A moan came from her throat as she used her tongue to wring a similar sound from Jett. Her hips lifted in invitation as Dylan found the little bud at the top of her sex with his tongue. Need twisted in her womb as he sucked her flesh into his mouth and flicked the tip of his tongue over it.

Pleasure ripped through her body as Dylan chuckled and sucked on her little bud as she drove Jett towards climax at the same time with her own lips. Jett gasped and gripped her hair as her fingers moved up and down his cock. His hips thrust his cock towards her as the first spurt of his seed hit her mouth. His fingers twisted in her hair as his hips bucked against her mouth. Jessica stroked the length of his cock as he grunted.

A second round of pleasure hit her brain as her own body tumbled into orgasm. Dylan held her hips in a solid grip as his tongue flicked over her clit making her cry out with the intensity of the pleasure. She wasn't sure who felt what, only that Jett's climax was as real to her as her own was and he in turn moaned as she cried out with pleasure.

"What was that?"

Jett grinned at her with a proud little twist of his lips that exposed his white teeth to her.

"When our minds are linked, the pleasure is shared."

"You're joking?"

He shook his head and smiled at her. Curiosity was suddenly too much for her. Jessica lifted her hand and curled her fingers around the solid length of cock. It was still hard and Jett sucked his breath in on a harsh note as she savored the feel of the weapon. He felt incredible. She ran her fingers from the base to the tip and back again. A wave of pleasure moved through her mind.

"Now that's too cool."

He grunted as he rolled back onto his back next to her on the bed. Jessica felt herself fill with confidence as she felt desire blaze from Dylan. She sat up as she reached for his length. Dylan gasped as he rolled onto his back. Jett's hands stroked her back as she licked the swollen head of Dylan's cock. She stroked and pulled on his cock as his breathing became labored. The way he floated inside her head showed her exactly what motions he craved.

She watched, fascinated, as his hips bucked and his face drew taut. She actually felt the orgasm build and break over his body. His staff erupted with a thick stream of seed that hit her hand as she continued stroking his sex until the last of the pulses subsided.

"Way weird. But still cool." Maybe she should be a little more freaked out over the telepathy but she really wasn't. It was more of a deep intimacy than what she would have thought mind reading to feel like. She couldn't tell what Dylan was thinking, just what he was feeling. He and Jett floated across her mind as she lay between them. Their skin connected, just as their thoughts did and it all felt so...complete.

That idea was a little too intense. Dylan's eyes opened to show her a look of pure determination. Her mouth went dry as she considered the promise burning behind those black eyes. He reached for her hand and captured it in his large one.

"Let's bathe."

The tone of voice he used made her shiver. It was so deep, Dylan made her feel like she was the entire focus of his attention. The complete devotion made her feel cherished.

Dylan pulled her behind him and smiled. Her fingers curled lightly into his grip betraying her growing trust. He suspected she would deny it loudly given the chance, but her body spoke clearly. He stepped into the water and pulled her down with him.

The water was warm. Jessica smiled as she sank down into it. It was exactly as warm as it had been during her bath but it sparkled bright and clean. These little touches of technology made things actually seem possible.

Two large hands gently cupped her breasts making her gasp. The two globes of flesh that had always seemed too large suddenly looked just right. They fit into Dylan's hands perfectly. He fell to his knees in the water bringing his head even with her nipples. Jessica licked her lips as she watched him open his mouth to taste her once again.

Jett was seated on the edge of the pool with just his legs in the water. His eyes were darkly intense as he watched Dylan suckle her. Her eyes were glued to the cock between his legs as it jerked and stiffened.

Dylan sucked a nipple into his mouth and used the tip of his tongue to stroke it. Jessica gripped his shoulders, as her head seemed to spin in a dizzy circle. Giving up seemed so simple, as well as very pleasurable. The idea of him filling her body with that hard cock started whispering through her brain as her passage began to throb with need. She wanted more than just climax, her body wanted to be filled and stretched around their hard cocks.

"What do you want, Jessica?" His hand gently squeezed her breast as he rose out of the water. It streamed down his chest in tiny rivulets that made him glisten. Jett curled his hand around his own erection and stroked its length, making her even more acutely aware of how good the hard flesh would feel inside her.

"Kiss me." She was suddenly impatient for the taste of his mouth. Jessica rose on her toes as she met Dylan halfway. Her lips opened immediately for the thrust of his tongue, and she sent her own to mingle and taste his.

His hands settled onto her hips and lifted her until she ended up on the edge of the pool.

"Open your legs for me."

Every touch seemed so intense. She was addicted to the way her body craved more from him. With a soft moan of surrender she let her knees separate and open.

"Put your hands on the floor."

Jessica flattened her palms on the cool stone floor. The position thrust her breasts forward. Dylan licked first one then the second nipple before he trailed tiny kisses down her body.

He pushed her thighs further apart as his hands gripped and held her hips in place. She watched wide-eyed as he hovered over her exposed sex.

He pressed a soft kiss against her bare mound and she jerked with sharp sensation. His tongue gently licked her folds from top to bottom before he found the little nub that was throbbing for attention. He circled it with slow motions before applying his lips to it in a deep suction that stole her ability to think.

The water moved as Jett left the pool and appeared behind her. His hands found her breasts as he kissed her throat.

Nothing mattered anymore. Jessica moaned and thrust her hips up, as she became a body driven by her need for release. Dylan sucked and licked, bringing her closer to a climax that was going to rip her in two.

Abruptly Dylan stood up. His eyes were relentless as they bore into hers. His hand captured the side of her face as he leaned down to softly growl.

"I did not bring you here to be my release-giver. You will bind with me, Jessica. Anything less I refuse."

He climbed from the water in one harsh movement. His eyes considered her flaming cheeks a second before he strode towards the door. Jett bit her neck before turning her face to his glare. "Bind with me, Jessica, and I will feed every one of your desires." He, too, climbed to his feet and walked towards the curtain. Both men simply grabbed their clothing and carried it with them as they left.

Her body screamed with hunger so great it became pain. They reached into her mind to touch that desire before they severed their connection with a swift blow. Jessica sank into the water as she tried to absorb their actions. Emotions were spinning out of control through her mind as her body twisted and yearned for more of their touch. The curtain swished down separating her completely from them.

"All you must do is ask, Jessica."

Jessica pulled her knees to her chest as she refused to invite them back. Her body screamed for their touch as her mind rebelled against how little willpower she appeared to have.

She ended up on the bed and the scent of her companions teased her nose as she closed her eyes.

# Chapter Five

## 🙤

Cole flexed his fingers and heard every knuckle pop. He knew what anger felt like but at that moment, cold fury was washing aside every other emotion as it flooded his brain.

"You sent my sister through the portal?"

"Get a grip, Somerton, did you think the battle was going to be won without sacrifice?"

Cole looked at Major Rinehart and kept his jaw tightly controlled. The hairs on the back of his neck tingled as the Major's eyes looked at him with some kind of twisted enjoyment.

"You should have kept them from seeing your own family. You knew what they were doing on our planet."

There was a snort of disgust from Rinehart before he turned and walked away. Cole stared at the man's back as he tried to make sense of the encounter. He never would have guessed that the major held any dislike for the Alcandians. Tonight, there wasn't anything but resentment filling the major's head. Cole considered the feeling as he moved towards the wormhole. Questions spun to mind as he noticed more sentries in place than before.

That tingle on his neck became a full attack of gut instinct. Something wasn't right but he stepped forward instead of investigating because the major was right about one thing.

It was his sister over there now.

\* \* \* \* \*

Her body actually hurt.

Jessica climbed out of the bed and rubbed her burning eyes. Her nap hadn't been restful. What she needed was a good long walk. Anything to get her mind off her body's screaming demands.

The curtain was still closed. Jessica lifted the edge of it slowly. No one appeared to be guarding her, so she slipped out and down the stairs. The hum of voices rose up from the main room but there was a second door right next to the stairs. She pressed on it hoping it led outside.

The panel dissipated in a golden shower of glitter the second she stepped towards it. Jessica stepped through it and watched it reappear with another glimmer of sparkles. The large stone courtyard lay in front of her. Men were walking along the stone-covered paths. Most were in groups talking and no one seemed to pay her any great deal of attention.

But there were no women. Jessica stepped forward at a good pace. She'd seen very few women in the hall of Dylan's house as well. But there didn't appear to be any shortage of men.

"Walking alone is an invitation to be stolen."

Jett was leaning against a large stone column. His eyes were hard little probes that hit her as she walked down the path. He straightened his body to its full height and continued to aim his disapproving look at her.

"Really? Well, I guess the next guy will just have to take a number and get in line behind you."

"Why does my concern anger you?"

Jessica considered Jett as he stood in her way. He'd crossed his arms across his chest. With his feet spread shoulder-width apart, he made a very effective roadblock. His jaw was tightly clenched as she caught the hint of an erection in the front of his pants.

"Most women on my planet consider themselves to be quite capable of providing for themselves. I don't need someone to take me out for a walk."

"Yet, there is much evidence to prove it is foolish for you to walk out alone even on your own world."

"Do you know very much about my home?"

"Aye. I have gone there often in my search for you."

His tone told Jessica that Jett didn't think very highly of Earth. It was still hard to think about her current location as a place actually not on her home planet's surface. Looking at the man in front of her, she tried to find something about him that would remind her that Jett was an alien. But he was every inch a perfect example of a man.

"I am your mate, Jessica. You will not expose yourself to capture."

"Fine. I'm going for a walk, so I guess you just invited yourself along."

She went right around the man. It was a gamble, but Jett only huffed under his breath before turning to fall into step beside her. His presence rubbed at her but she was just too happy to be outside. Anyway, maybe she should let him walk with her. She was on a foreign planet. She didn't even know what wildlife was poisonous. For all she knew, what looked like a squirrel might be as deadly as a rattlesnake.

Being ignorant bothered her worse than Jett's protective attitude. Jessica slid a look at her company to see that he was running his eyes over everything around them. He reminded her of Cole. Her brother always seemed to be looking for an attack.

"What did you mean about me risking capture?"

"Alcandians produce very few female offspring. A woman of childbearing age that is unbound is quite rare."

"So, if you really are so advanced, why hasn't science rectified that little problem?"

Jett stopped and raised his lips into a little grin. He tilted his head to the right. Jessica shrugged and decided to follow his lead. She didn't know where she was going anyway. A set of stone steps led them up into another stone-covered courtyard.

"All species are genetically coded to revert to one gender. In the case of Alcandians, our genetic code is trying to evolve into a male race. Unless human science intervenes, your own race will become solely female."

A tiny shiver went down her spine. She'd actually heard something about that on a newscast once. Some study on genetics, but Jett stated it as fact and that made it that much more believable. Jessica shook her head and tried to fend off the feeling she was really trapped.

"That doesn't tell me why you haven't fixed the problem."

"Interfering in the genetic code was something we tried. It almost destroyed our race."

"There's a great deal of debate raging on Earth about it right now."

Jett gave her a hard nod of agreement before he took her around a corner. Jessica completely forgot about him as her eyes took in the wonder in front of her.

Six waterfalls all cascaded down from a high cliff. The sunlight streamed through the water making it shimmer with all the colors of the rainbow. The air was full of mist that rose as the water hit the ground. There was a large lake formed by the water before it ran off into a river. Finding this right next to the modern building was amazing.

There were men swimming. Their heavily muscled arms cut through the water, as they seemed to glide across the shining surface.

"So nothing positive came from your genetic research?" Jessica bent down to trail her fingers in the water. It was crisp and cold just like any mountain river. Jett leaned against a large tree as his eyes made yet another pass over their surroundings.

"Many advantages were gained, but they were paid for with a great deal of suffering. If you experiment with genetics on a vegetable all you get are unusable products. When the product is a babe it is not so simple to dispose of it."

"I see your point."

A grin appeared on Jett's face. She recognized the little expression now. Dylan lifted the corner of his mouth exactly like that when he was feeling arrogantly superior.

"That doesn't mean I agree with this whole claiming thing, but it's nice to get some details on why Alcandians do things the way they do."

"Dylan will change your mind. I will enjoy helping him do it."

Jessica stood up. Her enjoyment of the water was abruptly destroyed. The arrogance of these people was amazing. She couldn't change the fact that they did seem to have the ability to physically capture her, but her mind was her own. She wasn't about to transform into some simpering sex slave.

"I doubt that. I'm not going to let my sex drive corner me into any kind of promises—that's what dildos were created for."

Jett threw his head back and laughed. His wide shoulders shook with his amusement before he aimed his eyes back at her.

"The Alcandian male brain is extremely sensitive to the pheromones of his mate." Jett's dark eyes dropped to her chest and lingered over the little points her nipples were raising through her jacket. "Your body craves our union as much as we do. The only rod that will sate you is mine and Dylan's."

Jessica shook her head—just because her nipples were tight didn't mean there was a single shred of truth to the whole crazy idea of her being someone's mate. Even if there were valid reason for Jett and Dylan to enter a union with one female.

91

"When it comes to mating, the body is very basic. The male becomes aggressive and the female often attempts escape."

"I just went for a walk!"

"Nay. You are aroused. I can even smell your scent. We are twice as responsive to your growing fever."

"That's nonsense." Jessica shifted away from Jett and crossed her arms over her chest. Her nipples sent up a ripple of sensation as she brushed them. Jessica let her teeth sink into her lower lip in frustration. All right, maybe she was a little...aroused. Who wouldn't be after men like Dylan and Jett had gotten naked with them? It was just human nature.

"It is fact, Jessica. A complex chemical reaction has begun inside your brain. In its milder forms it is simple lust. One of the advantages of our genetic experimentation was to remove the most primitive instinct to mate with multiple females. Once an Alcandian male finds his mate he will not rest until he conquers her."

"I'm human." Her words were whisper-soft. His words made too much sense.

"Which is why you resist. You still experience primitive lust. That is making it difficult for you to notice the difference immediately. Have you ever responded so strongly to any other male?"

She hadn't. Jessica felt her answer spring to mind instantly. Dylan could steal her breath with one of those hot kisses of his and she could have easily been thinking of her grocery list while Bryan kissed her. It had been pleasant but not completely spellbinding. The way Jett handled her breasts was the most erotic thing she'd ever felt. Between the two men there wasn't even a scrap of self-control. All she thought about was need and the two men eager to fill that empty ache between her thighs.

Jett suddenly raked her with eyes that blazed. He lingered over her breasts as he pushed away from his lazy position against the tree. He held out a single large hand to her.

"Come here, Jessica."

"You got that thought, I guess." His eyes flashed blue at her as he grinned and nodded.

His eyes had become twin flames as he listened to her response through their linked thoughts. He moved through her mind in a wall of flame that licked its way down her body. The desire they had left unsated rose to its yearning pitch as Jett moved forward to capture the hand she'd bound into a fist to keep from laying it in his.

"Your needs cry out to me, that is the way true mates should always be."

His body was solid as he caught her against it. She twisted as the warm scent from his skin made her passage ache for the hard thrust of the cock pressing against her belly.

"We will gladly give everything you desire, Jessica. All you must do is honor our union as well."

His mouth caught hers as she moaned with need. Jett pushed past her lips until his tongue stroked the length of hers. His hard erection throbbed against her, promising to fill the empty passage that screamed so loudly for his possession. But the truth was, she didn't want Jett, she wanted them both.

It was a shocking truth. Jessica ripped her body away from Jett as the warrior glared at her. He held his huge body in place as she watched him battle the urge to follow her.

"Soon, it will become undeniable."

"Go to hell!"

Jessica turned on her heel and took off. She didn't care if she did end up captured or getting bitten by something deadly. She would not be reduced to a mare in season. What kind of woman needed two men?

Guilt slammed into her head as Jett's words echoed through her skull. The shoe was on the other foot now! They were demanding that she step up and make a commitment to them. She had never considered being the one dragging her feet to the altar—maybe it was a whole lot easier to complain about what you didn't get from other people instead of looking at what you weren't willing to give.

Jessica wanted her needs filled but she wasn't willing to bind. Maybe Bryan wasn't such a jerk after all. That or she was cut from the same cloth.

Either way, Jett and Dylan had more self-control then she did...damn their luck!

* * * * *

There was nothing Jessica hated more than feeling uncertain. She didn't think the emotion had bothered her since she was thirteen, but in the last two days, it seemed like her closest companion. She picked up her feet faster as she tried to force her body to feel something other than arousal.

There were still pulses of longing running up and down her body. Her breasts swayed with her steps and the nipples brushed against the fabric of her jacket triggering more intense aches from them.

It was so very frustrating! She'd never been so aware of her breasts. Sure, she'd had a boyfriend or two who had shown her the basic pleasure that came from caresses, but this was completely different. It actually classified as an ache.

Jett trailed behind her as she once again quickened her pace. She felt surrounded. The need to run was almost overpowering.

A set of stairs caught her eyes and Jessica took them two at a time. It was a beautiful planet. The stone steps and walls gave it an old-world look that was comfortable. The little conveniences of technology made it almost too good to be true. Most housework seemed to have been eliminated. No beds to make, no bathtubs to scrub, you didn't even have to pass the food around the table.

Jessica stopped at the top of the stairs. She stared in fascination at the open field in front of her. There were at least three hundred men there. They were all engaged in a physical training exercise of some kind. It was a complex series of movements that made them push their bodies to the extreme. It resembled a martial arts class in its tight discipline, but the moves were blunt, harsh and deadly.

The temperature was rather mild, yet their bodies glistened with sweat. They were all bare-chested. Jessica searched them, looking for anyone who wasn't the very picture of perfection. There wasn't a single flabby tummy to be found. Each and every man was toned to top physical condition. They were also training with the ferocity of men who expected to use their bodies as weapons.

"Each man here is expected to be able to defend the Sinlar household. Our females are the most valuable possession we have."

"Sinlar?"

"Our family group—your Earth word might be clan."

One man abruptly broke the formation. His eyes caught hers as Jessica felt Dylan invade her mind with his presence. Jett stepped closer and Dylan's eyes moved over the other warrior before he gave a sharp nod of his head. He dropped back into the training routine in a quick fluid motion.

"You must never leave our chambers alone. The surrounding clans would risk the lives of their warriors to capture you."

Jessica frowned as she watched Dylan move. His body truly was a weapon, and he was ensuring it remained that way. She shivered as she considered his motives. It was survival of the fittest. He intended to defend his claim on her. The idea of being stolen suddenly took root in her brain as a truly horrible fate. The thought of not seeing Dylan or Jett again almost brought her to tears.

"But you said Alcandians had to find their true mates. If you are my mate why would anyone steal me?"

Jett's face transformed. She had seen him angry but this was fury. "Before a warrior touches his mate he can find relief with any female. It is a harsh truth that the body doesn't always need emotion to release its seed. Because we have touched your mind, you would not be able to bond with any other and they would use your body for relief."

"That's a charming idea."

"My heart would die without you, *renina*. Do not take foolish chances."

He was asking her. Jessica shifted her eyes over to look at Jett. His eyes glittered with the hunger she felt pulsing along her own skin. She couldn't seem to thrust him aside in favor of Dylan. Instead the two men were mixing inside her head like some combination that needed all three components in order to be complete.

His fingers settled on her chin to keep their eyes locked. He stepped closer, and with the closing of distance came the warm scent of his body. It triggered another wave of desire from her already needy body. The unmistakable flow of fluid went down the walls of her passage as she watched him lean towards her mouth again. The will to refuse his kiss dissipated into vapor as his firm mouth caught hers. She wanted those lips on hers. Tasting and sliding along her own lips until he pushed into her mouth to stroke her tongue.

She met him as her hand sought that length of black hair. Everything about him seemed strong. It was almost like she needed to touch him and share that strength.

"Your touch is worth waiting for, my *renina*."

The endearment was foreign but muttered in a husky tone that told her what it was. The fact that Jett didn't use the same words as Dylan made her tremble. They were both so different, yet part of the hunger that blazed inside her.

Jett watched her with a hard look as she moved further away. His fingers curled into tight fists as he forced himself to not follow her.

He wanted to. She felt his determination invade her mind as she struggled with recalling just why the relationship was wrong.

It all felt incredibly right. Her body was pulsing with a need that she'd never encountered before, pulsing and twisting in her belly until all she could see was the three of them entangled on that huge round bed.

Abruptly she turned and ducked around Jett. Her fingertips were suddenly sensitive as she imagined herself touching both of the firm chests being offered to her. Her nipples brushed against her coat again making her groan. This walk wasn't helping. Instead she found herself understanding Dylan's and Jett's logic.

Once you understood something it was far easier to agree with it. The word *accept* was right on the heels of that idea and she moved faster as she tried to keep it from settling into her brain.

The trail in front of her suddenly became blocked by another warrior. Jessica slowed her pace as she considered him. He was planted right in her path as she walked towards him. The wide set of his feet said the man wasn't interested in moving.

Jett's hand fell on her shoulder and stopped her dead in her tracks. His hand firmly held her in her position as he came beside her and stepped forward to greet the man. Jessica looked away from Jett's grip to see their company rapidly bearing down on them. Dressed in Alcandian clothing, she looked at the man twice before she realized exactly who she was looking at.

Her brother was absolutely furious.

"Where in the hell is Dylan?"

Jett stepped forward until he was standing within inches of Cole. Both men seemed to puff up their chests as they glared as each other.

"Dylan is training. I am Jett and serve as companion to Dylan. Jessica is our binding mate."

"Like hell! That's my sister."

"And she is our mate. An emissary should understand this. We have touched her mind."

"Excuse me." Jessica stepped around Jett and ignored the grunt of disapproval it earned her. Cole's face seemed to flush even hotter as he ran his eyes over her clothing. "You two can fight later."

Jett grunted again and Cole seemed eager to engage the man. Jessica grabbed her brother's arm and pulled him into step with her as she headed back towards the house.

"But first, you're going to explain a few things to me, Cole."

* * * * *

"Why are you so ticked off?" Jessica glared at her brother as he paced. He would stop and shoot furious looks at Jett before turning around to pace again. Back inside the bottom floor of Dylan's house, Jett had given them exactly twenty feet of space.

"Cole? Are you deaf? I think if anyone has the right to be mad, it's me."

Her brother stopped dead in his tracks and looked at her with a long face. His mouth twisted with unpleasantness as his eyes turned solemn.

"God, Jessica! I never thought they'd ever meet you. Much less choose you." Cole ran a hand through his hair before dropping into a chair next to her. Resignation settled over his face chilling her to the bone.

"Cole, you'd better start spilling some beans. I can't take any more of this guessing game."

"I'm sorry, Sis."

It was a flat statement. The finality of it made her stomach drop. Cole's face was deadly serious as he looked at her.

"Are you telling me this is some kind of done deal?"

"It's reality, Jessica." Her brother laced his fingers together before he very precisely invaded her mind. The contact startled her until Jessica realized the sensation was familiar.

"You're psychic?"

"Yes. Being my sister makes it highly likely you carry the same gene."

"You mean there's actual genetics to support it?"

Cole nodded before aiming a small grin at her. "The human population isn't willing to embrace the data. We've been working with the Alcandians to stabilize the gene pool on Earth. It isn't a simple process. But the rewards will be amazing. It goes beyond telepathy. I can control my immune system, influence metabolism, and choose my fertility level."

"Just like that?" Jessica snapped her fingers.

Cole grinned and shook his head. "Like anything, it takes practice."

"All right. So explain why I'm sitting here and why you're so mad about it."

The grin melted off her brother's face. "The downside of being able to choose my fertility is that I can only impregnate the female that my mind can psychically merge with. In other words, if I don't find a woman with the same psychic gene, I'm sterile. A little insurance policy, courtesy of Mother Nature."

Jessica shook her head but Cole grabbed her hand in a bruising grip.

"It's fact, Jessica. We either embrace it or face extinction."

"What do you mean?"

"Have you ever wondered why the marriage rate is dropping so rapidly? When only one member of a couple has the psychic gene, they lose interest in their partner and leave. In another generation, the birth rate will plummet to almost nothing."

"You're teaching in some underground program, aren't you?"

Cole nodded as his grin appeared again. Jessica let her mouth turn up in response. It was really a major relief to discover Cole wasn't just running around playing solider of fortune.

"It's a global net that will sweep aside national governments."

"Wow." That was an amazing idea. Life would certainly be better for everyone.

"The Alcandians have shared their knowledge in more areas than you can imagine, Sis. But they need our help too. Their race was affected by this evolution as well and it almost wiped them out."

Jett's words rose into bold print across her memory. The lack of women present suddenly impacted her with understanding.

"They want women."

Cole aimed sharp eyes at hers and held up a single finger.

"No, they want to be allowed to search Earth for their binding mates. Once they settle on a woman, if there is something that prevents the union, the males will spend the rest of their lives celibate."

Cole's hands grasped her shoulders in an almost painful grip.

"So will the female."

"Bull!"

Cole's face filled with arrogant knowledge. He didn't yell back at her, but Jessica wished he had. If they were both yelling, it was a fight and so much easier to believe they might both be wrong. Instead, she felt like a child throwing a tantrum over something that could not be changed.

"You're no virgin, Cole."

A corner of her brother's mouth twitched up. "I haven't found my binding mate, Sis. The problem on Earth is men try to make relationships work when it's not the right woman."

She didn't like the smug little smile that covered her brother's face now. He looked at her with understanding and that wasn't what she wanted to see. His smile faded as she refused to swallow his logic.

"Fine, do you want to go back to Bryan?"

"I broke up with him."

"Maybe you need to think about why you did that, Sis." Cole turned and began walking away. He seemed to know the path well, making it far too simple to consider living on Alcandar. It looked like her brother was quite comfortable here.

"You know something, Sis? Love doesn't show up on schedule." Her brother's lips were back in that grin. "You're not the first woman who has had to adjust her life to accommodate a marriage."

"They kidnapped me and your buddies helped."

Her brother's face went stone-hard. "I know, but it isn't the same thing to them. Alcandians consider it much more honest to declare their intentions before any touching happens."

"That sounds medieval." But not horrible. Jessica huffed as she considered the fact that Dylan and Jett weren't interested in anything but a permanent relationship. It was certainly a different tone from the dating scene back home.

"It's considered honorable for the female." Cole shrugged his shoulders before looking back at her. "Dylan and Jett have been companions since their youth. They have always expected to share one mate between them. To their way of thinking, humans do it oddly."

"Mom is going to skin you alive if she ever hears you talking like that."

Cole grinned like a little boy with his hand in a cookie jar. "But she'd be delighted to have me jumping into a marriage on the first day I met that special girl."

Oh would she! There was a bond between her and her brother—they both tried to aim their mother's grandbaby need at the other sibling.

"Why don't you give it a fair chance, Sis?"

"That would depend on what I'm giving the chance to, Cole. There's more to life then hot sex."

But with her brother's information came the tempting desire to accept the current dilemma as a different slant on life. Just because a culture wasn't your own didn't mean it was wrong. Oh brother! At this rate, she'd be indulging her vivid fantasies before the sun rose tomorrow morning!

# Chapter Six

ဢ

It was so much to take in, yet incredibly simple to understand. Jessica went right back up the stone steps that led to Dylan's chamber as she turned the information over in her head.

Jett and her brother were currently trying to stare each other down.

Was she really destined to be unhappy in relationships? Was that her problem with Bryan? Could it really be blamed on her chromosomes?

"Your brother has explained things to you?"

Jessica whipped around to see Dylan frowning deeply at her but hope burned in his eyes. Temptation urged her to feed that hope and fling herself into the relationship being offered.

"Cole had a lot of interesting things to say." God, the man defined sexy. Her brain kept trying to dissolve into mush when he got close to her. She hissed under her breath with frustration.

Dylan smiled. He could feel her in every cell of his body. The sensation was sharply acute and he savored it. Color flooded her cheeks as she battled to ignore her rising need. It wasn't passion. What heated their blood was a fever that would let them join in the deepest forms of ecstasy.

But the hesitation in her bothered him immensely. Very soon, his control would be unable to hold back his need to possess her. Her body would yield to him. Dylan was confident but he wanted more.

"Why are you angry?" Dylan's eyes snapped with his voice as he followed her shifting steps across the room.

"I'm frustrated."

Dylan grunted and crossed his arms.

"I don't understand why you didn't explain to me what my brother just told me. On Earth we communicate with our mates."

"Talking is not what burns across my mind when I am near you. The scent of your body near drives me insane. I do not just want your body, Jessica, I want you and no other for the rest of my years!"

His eyes flared with determination as she felt her body surge forward with delight over his words. Maybe details weren't all that important.

"So where does Jett fit into this whole thing?"

Dylan stepped closer, making her shift away. "When a man becomes a warrior, he finds other men that he can bind with mentally. Jett is my brother in all things. He is a part of me just as you are. You and I would be incomplete without him. We are brothers and the attraction of one becomes the obsession of the other."

The conversation was heading straight back towards sex again. Jessica searched her brain for a topic that wouldn't have her listening to her body so intensely. She looked at the hard glitter sitting in Dylan's eyes and frantically tried to engage her brain.

"What do you do?"

His forehead creased with confusion.

"For a living. I mean, you don't spend all day training, do you?"

Dylan nodded with satisfaction.

"I am an investigator of disturbance. Jett is my partner."

"You're a cop?"

"It bears some similarities to your culture's police force. Yet my duties are confined to uncovering the facts."

Great. So she wouldn't be complaining to the local law enforcement about being kidnapped.

"Your brother is also attached to this manner of work. As his sister, you are an excellent choice for my mate."

"So what if I'm just not ready for binding?"

Dylan pulled her into his embrace as his eyes flared with determination. "Do not say such foolish things," he hissed at her in a low growl. "Open your mind and I will enjoy showing you exactly how ready you are."

Desire flowed in a thick stream from his mind into hers. Jessica moaned softly as it swiftly overwhelmed her. But it became more than just Dylan, her body rose into a fever pitch of yearning that rejoiced as he appeared in her head again. Unity flowed around them until she wasn't sure where she ended and Dylan began. His eyes glittered above hers as he pressed his body along hers. His fingers stroked her cheek as his eyes glittered. "We have searched for years for you. Do you feel our completeness? Your body shivers just as I do. Once Jett is here, there will be nothing but pleasure."

His mouth caught her as he bent her backwards across his arm. Jessica clung to the shoulders her eyes had so greedily stared at. He felt so good. There had to be something wrong about the relationship. Instead her blood surged forward on a wave of heat so intense it burned her.

Her feet left the floor and Jessica sighed with approval. It felt so right! Dylan felt so right. It didn't make sense at the moment, but she wasn't interested in figuring anything out!

All that mattered was the intense need to get rid of her clothing. Her fingers traced the rigid muscles of his arms as Dylan laid her in the center of his bed. His fingers popped the twin buttons of her jacket and separated the edges to bare her breasts.

His face was so approving of her. Jessica felt her mouth lift into a smile. No one had ever made her feel so beautiful before. Dylan cupped her breasts in hands that lightly shook.

"You are perfection." His fingers brushed her nipples making her jump as a bolt of pleasure raced towards her belly. "Tell me what you like."

His command was so empowering. Jessica licked her lips as she considered being able to tell this massive man what to do. Images sprang into full color as she thought about how much pleasure he'd brought her with his mouth. But her clothing scratched her heated skin. Suddenly she simply wanted to watch his face as she displayed her body to him again.

"I want to take these clothes off."

"As I watch?"

Her belly twisted with the deep sound of his voice. His eyes cut into hers as his fingers brushed her nipples again. Power shifted between them as Jessica found herself asking to be allowed out of his embrace. There was certainly no way she could move if Dylan didn't let her go.

His finger traced a line to her chin and raised her face to his. "Will you disrobe for me, *heloni?*"

"Yes." Whisper-soft, Jessica wasn't even sure it was her voice. Something inside was transforming her into a female who believed in her own attractiveness. She seemed to feed off the feelings Dylan was projecting into her mind and found herself believing in her ability to please such a stunning male as him.

He grinned like a boy and rolled back onto the bed. But he didn't stop, instead, he rolled right over the opposite side and striped his clothing from his body in exactly three seconds. That magnificent body stood facing her a moment before he dropped back onto the bed and rolled onto his side. His eyes were glued onto the drooping edges of her jacket. Jessica rolled her shoulders and the garment slipped easily off.

She wasn't thinking about what she was doing anymore. Dylan's face fascinated her. His eyes sharpened with anticipation as she sent her fingers towards the waistband of her pants. While lust played its part in the blaze of heat simmering in those black depths, the look lacked the one-sidedness she'd grown to expect from men.

This man wanted her. Not just the wet passage between her legs. As she slipped the fabric down her legs, Jessica found herself believing that he would have completely ignored any other woman in the room. His eyes were devoted to her.

It was a silly, emotional idea. But it clung to her as Dylan patted the surface of his bed. She licked her lips as she contemplated the surge of heat that spilled down her body. The walls of her passage heated as she felt them slick with her own fluids.

He hadn't touched her. Instead the hunger that he'd left burning in her body that morning renewed its grip on her flesh. There wasn't enough strength in her mind to resist the need pulsing from her belly. The thick staff pointing towards her promised to feed the growing desire that twisted around her.

Suddenly he groaned as he listened to her thoughts. It was like they were two mirrors aimed at each other. The reflections hit and collided, multiplying the images until nothing else existed.

He stood and Jessica watched that magnificent body close in on her. Once again his male body overwhelmed her, but this time she flung herself into the wave of heat. It sizzled along her nerve endings as she twisted her hands into his hair. The hard wall of his chest made her purr as her body melted and yielded against it.

His lips caught hers as Jessica turned her head to fit against him. Her feet rose from the floor as Dylan held her with one solid arm across her waist. Their bare skin met and she felt the shiver that rose across her in response. One huge hand captured the back of her head as his tongue thrust deeply into her mouth.

She twisted in his embrace as wave after wave of pleasure collided with each other. Heat rose even higher as his tongue continued to trace the length of her own.

The hard thrust of his cock burned into her thigh as she sent her tongue towards his. He moved and the bed suddenly caught her weight. But Dylan didn't cover her body. Instead he rolled until his back was on the soft surface of the bed. His hand caught each of her thighs and spread them until she sat atop his hips. A harsh gasp left her lips as the folds of her sex opened and gripped the length of his erection. The hard rod of flesh lay pulsing against the spread opening to her body. Her body screamed for her to lift her bottom and complete the intimacy she craved, the walls of her passage clenching with the need to hold that hard cock.

"Your body is so wet, *heloni*. Welcome me into your passage." His voice was a bare whisper but it was cut with the hard need that drew his face taut. The hands on her thighs shook with just the hint of a tremor as he used his iron will to allow her the choice.

His fingers found the hard nubs of her nipples. Jessica purred as her breasts burst into pleasure. Not once had she ever believed the globes of flesh could hold such delight. She moaned as the walls of her passage clenched again. She felt so empty, so desperate to be filled. What she craved was to have Dylan's hard length pressed into the delicate tissues of her spread body.

She rose on her thighs and felt his cock spring up towards her. The hard tip of it probing for the opening to her body. His hand left her breasts to grip her hips and hold her above his body.

One hard inch of his weapon entered her, stretching the walls that screamed for more but she caught a moan as the skin protested the invasion. Caught between need and blunt possession, Jessica hesitated. She raised her eyes to find his black ones glittering with strain. His face was cut into deep grooves as he suppressed the need to thrust deeply into her.

The sacrifice hit her as tender as she watched him battle for control. His need flowed between them like lava as she struggled to lift her body.

"Dylan, help me."

"Help you how?"

He growled the words as his eyes refused to relent. He wanted her to demand him. Put into spoken word the need that clawed at her. She lowered back onto the hard length of his cock but his hands held her in the same position. This time the small allowance of penetration made her body burn with pleasure, but she wanted all of his length. His hands refused to allow the deep plunge that her body urged her to take.

"Please."

She didn't care anymore. Her body had never demanded she indulge its hunger before. The reasons and logic of the situation just didn't matter! She'd spent endless hours trying to cultivate this same reaction to men who had only inspired the most tepid of sexual responses.

"I want you, Dylan."

His hands released and Jessica let her body plunge towards the staff it craved. Pain slashed along the path of penetration as her body split to allow the intrusion. Dylan lifted her and moved her back onto his length with gentle movements before she sucked in a deep breath and the pain receded.

His eyes glittered with hunger as he watched her face intently. His mind still caught her every emotion as his pleasure bled into hers. Her passage clenched the solid length of his cock and urged her to move. Jessica lifted her body and let it fall back onto the rod that stretched her even further as her body relaxed and opened for him.

Pleasure spiked into her belly as she repeated the motion. His hands helped her rise as he bucked and thrust beneath her. Jessica gasped as her body drew into a knot that tightened with each thrust from his body. She rose to gain another hard penetration from that burning erection. The walls of her passage clenched and gripped his length as pleasure shattered inside her in a shower of light that stole every last thought from her head.

All that mattered was the pulse of his length buried inside her.

Her pleasure stole his breath. Dylan snarled as he surged from the bed and spread her body beneath his. The scent of her release fired his blood as his hips drove his cock deep between her thighs. The wet sound of his penetration made his chest rumble with a low growl of approval. She gasped and clung to his shoulders as her bottom lifted for his thrusts.

"Aye, *heloni*, match me, lift for me." His teeth nipped her neck as he thrust harder into her soft body. Her cries fired his blood as his hips demanded complete surrender to his rhythm. Dylan wanted to ride her until her voice died from too many cries.

"Tell me again you want to go back to the planet of your birth."

His body tightened as her passage gripped his cock. Pulling and milking his rod as she once again gave in to climax. He erupted inside her body as he thrust deep into her wet softness. His voice was harsh as he emptied his seed against her womb. Satisfaction followed the burst of primal pleasure as Dylan listened to the moan of rapture that escaped from his mate. No words of denial formed in her thoughts as she lay spread and welcoming beneath his body.

"Tell me any human ever made you sound like I just did." Pulling his cock from her body he smoothed a hand over one thigh. "Tell me, *heloni*, that you want to leave our bed."

She couldn't do it. Her lips refused to form the words that would reject him. Every fiber in her echoed contentment as his eyes demanded and dared her to speak a single word of rejection.

"I don't know what I want." Just him. It seemed the only thing she did know that she wanted in that moment. The scent of his body, the firm muscle under her fingertips.

"I do. You want us the way we desire you. It burns as strongly in your belly as it does us. Think how much more intense it will be when Jett completes our union."

He rolled off her body and took her with him. One strong hand molded and tucked her along that hard length of muscle-bound maleness.

"You belong next to me, Jessica. Yet I will be most happy to prove it again do you not require rest."

She froze in place as her body leapt with the idea. Jessica pulled a deep breath into her lungs as she tried to find the way to chastise her own wanton flesh. Two days ago, life had made sense. Now she was in bed with a man who stole her breath and also her ability to think.

A wave of fatigue washed over her as her body began to whisper its longing for more of the pleasure Dylan had produced. Her fingers rested on the hard plane of his chest and the sensitive endings wandered through the crisp hair that felt incredibly masculine.

Each breath pulled his male scent into her lungs where it confirmed her notice of his strength. There were deep, hidden places inside her that clamored for approval of his presence there next to her. The only thing missing was Jett. Her skin didn't want to be covered with clothing, she wanted to be between them both.

That idea followed her into sleep as Dylan grinned with full approval. He stroked her head as her breath deepened and the curtain hanging in the doorway moved. Jett ran his eyes over Jessica's face before he aimed his hungry eyes away from the temptation of her bare body.

\* \* \* \* \*

Dylan was gone.

Jessica reached across the bedding and frowned as her fingers found the trace of body heat still clinging to the sheets. She wasn't sure if her disgruntlement was aimed at the fact that Dylan had left her or the idea that she'd woken up within seconds of the man leaving her side.

But the covers were tucked around her shoulders making her lips lift into a silly smile. Bryan had certainly never taken the time to worry about her comfort. Of course, the man had always left the second she refused to go any further than oral sex.

Dylan was so different. Pushing the covers aside, Jessica eyed the bathing pool. She cast a quick glace at the curtain that covered the doorway and made a quick trail towards the inviting warm water.

The moment of privacy was going to be indulged in!

Jessica sank down into the water and sighed. She was sore. The heat eased the discomfort as she swam in a small circle around the pool. The night played across her thoughts like a favorite movie.

Jessica felt a blush stain her face. She'd wanted the man so much it almost frightened her. It certainly knocked her off balance. Dylan had walked into her life and just set up camp! The chase had been almost nonexistent. Her defenses swept aside by her own desire.

Standing up, Jessica went looking for her clothing. She expected the curtain to open any second with any number of Dylan or Jett's family and today, she was going to greet them dressed.

The jacket dress was really quite comfortable. The top of it cupped and supported her breasts better than any bra she'd ever owned. It didn't leave the red marks on her skin like the elastic straps of her normal underwear did.

The bed had already made itself as Jessica turned to look at the bathing pool. That too was clean as a mountain spring.

There wasn't even a tiny puddle left on the stone tile from were her feet had touched the smooth surface.

Well, women certainly didn't spend their days cleaning here. But that left her wondering just what she was going to do. Dylan might be the answer to her sexual fantasies but that wouldn't be enough to build a life around.

Jessica stood for a moment as she considered the idea of actually living on Alcandar. Her mind had been so focused on escape until now. She looked back at the bed and the clear reminder that at least on this planet, she'd found one thing that Earth had never seemed to grant her.

Dylan was certainly, and without a doubt, a man. No stupid games to get sex without strings. Instead, he'd brought her home, announced his intention to bind with her and introduced her to his mother.

She shook her head but emotion rose up even as she tried to deny it. He was a man. One who had bid farewell to games and took her very seriously.

Should she really be so worried about the details? Maybe not. Having Bryan ask her politely to dinner and playing the understanding date hadn't turned her blood into liquid heat. Her pride tried to rear its head again but Jessica just looked at the bed once more.

But going out and finding out what this world held for her future might be a good step to take, before she got anywhere near that amazing body Dylan had again.

* * * * *

Today, the bottom floor of the house was full of men but they didn't turn to stare at her. Jessica considered the long tables where men sat in groups as they ate and talked. A few even had some type of card game going. A few looked up as she moved past them but it was more an awareness of movement that caught their attention. Their heads moved up and their eyes took in details before returning to their game.

They were warriors. Each one trained to deal with attack. They didn't trust anyone walking near them and noticed her out of their trained instinct to survive. The fact that they quickly dismissed her brought a small smile to her lips. Acceptance from the group was a compliment.

It collided with her earlier idea of living here and made it harder to dismiss the notion as ridiculous. Dylan's people might be a lot of things but they were not beneath her.

Dylan brushed her mind making her jump. Several heads rose to investigate her jerky motions. Jessica turned her head to find Dylan sitting across the room. Her cheeks lit with a blush as she looked at the full lips of the man who had shared her bed. He lifted his hand in invitation as the men watching her suddenly grinned with knowing looks.

Jessica held her head high as those smiles gave way to low male amusement. She crossed the hall as each and every man took the moment to inspect her flaming face. But she stopped as she caught the eyes of the only male not amused by her blush.

Jett's eyes glittered with unmistakable hunger as he watched her. His eyes moved down her body with that same sharp intensity she had come to expect from Dylan. It was bold. His eyes returned to hers as he reached out to touch her thoughts.

Strength moved through her thoughts as Jett firmly let her feel his presence. Her body reacted with stunning force. Her breasts lifted and swelled as the nipples drew into twin points that stabbed into the front of her jacket.

The reaction was bluntly obvious to her now. A firm grin sat on Jett's face as he lowered his eyes to her hard nipples and back to her face. Arrogance was written in his eyes. Jessica looked at Dylan to see a smug look of approval to her reaction to the other warrior.

*He is my brother in all things.*

Dylan's words hit her in that moment as she looked at the very real evidence that the two men did intend her to be their mate. The idea was so surrounded by taboo that she stepped back from the table as she tried to wrap her mind around the idea of two men being acceptable. Maybe she had indulged in a few fantasies about the three of them but walking towards their table felt like a declaration of intent. The fluid seeping down the walls of her passage shouted for her to invite Jett back upstairs with her.

Both men rose from the table, their bodies hard and strong and impossibly attractive to her. Inside her was a female screaming for the ultimate possession of both superior males. Her mind rebelled at the idea as she tried to force herself to recall why having two men was wrong.

She turned on her heel and left. She thrust both men from her mind as she hurried down the aisle. Ignoring the frowns of the warriors, she continued on and tried to ignore the clamoring of her body to stop and yield.

The bright morning sunlight did stop her. Dylan and Jett were sitting at that table with frustration eating them alive. Jessica hissed under her breath. A pair of brutes running her to ground she could have detested. If they had yanked her into their arms and overpowered her senses, she could long for her freedom despite her passion.

But the power of choice disarmed her completely. They didn't just want her, they wanted to be her choice.

And her heart wasn't interested in listening to a single thing her pride had to say.

\* \* \* \* \*

"You must be Jessica."

Jessica rounded on the feminine voice.

"I am Zeva."

She stood for a moment as Jessica looked at her. Dark, long hair was pulled back from her eyes. The long coat-dress looked completely normal on the woman as Jessica found the dark black eyes smiling at her. There was something familiar about the shape of her face.

"I'm Jett's sister."

"Does everyone just jump into each other's thoughts around here?"

The woman laughed deeply before she lifted her hands into the air.

"It does have advantages, you know. But I guessed that one."

Jessica listened to her stomach growl as she shook her hand again. "Is there anywhere to get food around here beside back there?"

Zeva shot a hot look at the hall behind Jessica. "Men and women do not eat together here, except on special occasions. Come on, I'll show you the women's hall."

Oh, now there was a bit of information. Jessica frowned as she followed Jett's sister.

"So why didn't Jett or Dylan tell me that?"

Zeva turned and gave her a sly smile. "When a mate goes into the men's hall it is to issue an invitation. The men like to keep that a little secret until after the binding ceremony."

"I just bet they do."

Zeva laughed and shrugged. "Warriors—you can't fault their enthusiasm."

There was another building right next to the one she'd come to think of as Dylan's. A hallway connected the two but Zeva walked through one of the door panels that shimmered into glitter as the woman touched it.

"This is the women's hall." Zeva rolled her large dark eyes as she smiled at Jessica. "This is where we come for a little female companionship and some distance from male opinion."

"Zeva!"

Paneil appeared with the first frown that Jessica had ever seen on the woman's face. She aimed her disapproval at her daughter as Jessica tried not to smile.

"Your brother has done nothing wrong."

"No, he hasn't. I thought Jessica would like to see the women's hall." Zeva rolled her eyes and jerked her head at Jessica. "Food is this way."

Paneil aimed a bright smile at Jessica, making her hurry to catch up with Zeva. The younger woman seemed a little more willing to share real information and she wasn't about to let her get away.

Jessica stared at the mystery food before simply picking one up at random. Starvation wasn't picky, besides she had no clue what anything was. She was going to have to begin tasting the local fare somewhere. She sat down next to Zeva on a bench that also included a soft pad unlike the bare wooden ones in the men's hall.

"Why was your mother mad?"

"She thinks I should leave you hanging on my brother's arm until the binding ceremony has passed. She's eagerly anticipating a grandbaby to spoil."

Jessica snorted as she stuffed a chunk of food into her mouth. The flavor wasn't bad as she chewed it and looked up to find Zeva grinning at her.

"My mother is very happy with her binding mates and thinks I am overly stubborn." Zeva's eyebrows rose as she whispered her words to keep them from drifting to the other women sitting near by. They were being watched by most of them. Jessica's took a moment to look at the room. All ages of women and girls filled it. There were babies and adolescents and grandmothers. It was a relief to discover something on the planet that wasn't dominated by males. But there was still only maybe a third of the number that inhabited the male hall.

"So, you aren't bound?"

The word wasn't as awkward to say as she had thought it might be. In fact, Jessica was finding too many ideas easier to swallow this morning.

"To my mother's complete disappointment."

Jessica laughed. Some things were universal. Her own mother was forever dropping hints about grandbabies and the clock ticking. Looking back around the room, Jessica considered the faces of these women. They looked as happy as her own friends back on Earth. There weren't the dejected stares of humiliated possessions.

"Do all these women have two binding mates?"

"Some have three."

Jessica blinked at Zeva as the woman shrugged.

"Some men have more than one companion. They end up binding with the same woman or fighting over her. How do you make do with only one man? Isn't that frustrating?"

Zeva seemed to find the idea of one man just as alarming as Jessica found the thought of both Jett and Dylan.

"Frustrating how?"

"A female can have multiple climaxes, while a male is limited to one before he has to recover."

Zeva's words sparked an image in her mind that caused her belly to tighten. Dylan had wrung incredible pleasure from her body last night, if Jett had been there as well...good grief.

Zeva offered her a naughty smile. "As I said, there are advantages."

Maybe. Jessica found the entire day looking better now that her stomach wasn't growling.

"Well, I'd better get moving." Zeva stood as Jessica considered the woman. Jett's sister smiled before she stepped away from the table.

"Do you have a job?"

"Doesn't everyone?"

Jessica frowned. She felt like she stood outside the circle and hadn't even figured out yet that she needed to shoulder her way into it. For that matter, her own life might be crumbling back on Earth. She hadn't called in to her boss and after three days, her employer was bound to be more than a little ticked at her disappearance.

Then again, maybe not. Whoever Cole worked with, they tied up details rather well. That interview note had certainly fooled her into walking right into the trap.

But the idea of life on Alcandar being similar to her own brought her comfort level up another notch. Jessica chewed on her lip as she walked towards the door panel. The place became more likeable with each passing day.

Dylan was still arrogant and Jett his mirror image but that might just be a lesson in being careful what she wished for. She had longed for a man who would want the whole thing. Dylan and Jett were demanding it.

But what was she going to do when Jett entered his own demand to the equation?

Jessica felt the blood in her veins heat and speed up as she considered that huge bed holding all three of them. Earth taboos spun through her thoughts as she considered the fact that Alcandians considered the threesome a legal and even moral union.

The scariest thought she'd ever encountered was the idea creeping into her brain that maybe, she might just like Alcandian life better than Earth.

# Chapter Seven

## ജ

"Why did they threaten to shoot me if I talked about Alcandar?"

Cole jumped and spun around with his hands already rising to defend himself. His eyes sharpened as recognition flashed across them.

Jessica grinned and tossed her hair as she waited. So overwhelmed by the constant presence of either her intended mates or their mothers, she'd forgotten to think through some of the details.

"Answer me, Cole. These are your friends. If I can't refuse this binding thing then no one would bother to threaten to shoot me."

She was right and knew it. If threats were being handed out prior to stepping in that wormhole, then somewhere along the line, there was a possible return trip.

"You don't want to know."

Her eyes flared open as rage erupted in them.

"Try again, Cole. What's the big deal in telling me anyway? I'm already here."

Her brother considered her with dark eyes before he nodded his head. He wasn't a man who shared information easily.

"You can refuse to bind."

His words didn't fill her with elation. They should have. Jessica was annoyed with her fickle emotions as they whined at her to toss away the very idea of leaving Jett and Dylan.

"How?"

Cole grunted as his face drew taut with distaste. "There will be a final ceremony tomorrow. You bind with them or publicly denounce their ability to fulfill your needs."

Warning crept up her spine as she watched her brother's face grow even harsher. "How is that done?"

"You prove it."

Jessica propped her hands onto her hips and scowled at her brother. Cole cussed before lifting his hands in defeat.

"You offer your body to any of the warriors present. When they sexually please you, Dylan and Jett will renounce you and allow you to return to Earth."

She wanted to ask if he was joking. The dead serious look on his face told her he wasn't. Her brain instantly rejected the idea of anyone touching her but Jett and Dylan.

Unreal!

Now she was thinking of them together? Concern was wiggling its way into her mind as she even thought about finding a way to leave them. Tender feelings seemed to have emerged inside her and the idea of shaming the two warriors made her stomach twist.

She couldn't do it. But Cole's continued scrutiny made her temper explode and his jaw seemed a perfect target. Her fingers balled into a fist as her shoulder tightened just the right amount.

Cole jumped out of her range as a small grin appeared on his face. It was an expression born from their childhood and somehow it broke through the mask of the serious man who had been talking to her.

"Spoilsport."

He winked as he left on long strides. Jessica watched as her brother followed a growing stream of warriors as they headed for the practice fields. Twice a day they went like clockwork.

The exercise period was going to give her far too much time to think about Dylan and Jett and the bed big enough to hold them all.

\* \* \* \* \*

The level of fitness absolutely amazed her. Jessica leaned over the half wall of her chamber. Below her were only a dozen or so warriors but it still made her shake her head.

Humans would pay to come to Alcandian just for the health benefit. Women would line up for the chance to be claimed by any of the men sitting below her.

Was she really fated to belong here? It was an enormous idea. One that should have fallen under the term "fairy tale". Instead Cole's words echoed inside her head as she looked at one warrior sitting below her.

On Earth, he would have been her dream man. Dark, rugged, tall and built. She watched him lift a chunk of bread to his lips and bite off a mouthful. His jaw worked with hard movements as he chewed. She watched the man next to him but nothing stirred inside her. Not even a tiny spark of lust inspired by the sheer brawn of them. Both of them were what she used to be attracted to. Instead all she noticed today was the fact that they were both in prime condition.

"Jessica? It's Zeva. May I enter?"

"Sure."

The Alcandian woman slid her hand under the curtain and lifted it. She grinned as she caught Jessica leaning over the wall.

"I love the upper-floor rooms." She leaned out to look at the warriors.

"Of course mine doesn't have the same view."

"Where do you live?"

Zeva grinned as she came back into the chamber. "In the women's building. Only bound females are allowed in this hall. Come on, I'm starving."

Jessica followed Zeva down the stairs. All cooking seemed to be done as a community event. Separate families didn't provide for themselves, instead food was produced and shared as a community. With the higher level of technology, there weren't even dirty dishes to quibble over.

"What do you do, Zeva? I mean as a job?"

"I teach girls defense arts." Jett's sister stopped at the bottom of the stairs and smiled at her. "I'll be happy to take you to see my studio. In fact, I'm sort of hoping you might be interested in some work. Our contracts are a disaster. Only women can teach there and I could really use another body."

They stepped into the sunshine as the door panel shimmered and dissipated. The courtyard was beginning to fill with men as they headed in for the noon meal.

"As soon as the binding ceremony has passed you will be overwhelmed by offers of work. Just remember I asked first."

"What kind of work?"

Zeva smiled as she pointed at the courtyard. "All kinds. The men train a lot and that leaves a great deal of life for us women to manage. I guess the real question would be what do you like to do?"

"So housewifing isn't the only position for women?"

"It can be, if you like. Some females adore young children." Zeva smiled as she looked at her. "I like all my students but confess I prefer to teach girls the best."

"Zeva."

A large shadow blocked the sun as a warrior stepped into their path. Zeva snapped into deadly form as she faced the huge male. Fury was etched into the woman's face as she actually bared her teeth at the man.

"Get lost, Ravid."

Sparks seemed to fly from their eyes as some mental battle ensued. The huge warrior tried to step closer but Zeva suddenly hooked Jessica's arm and sent her tumbling into the warrior's chest.

Ravid's reflexes were as lightning-fast as Jett's. His arms caught her as her face went sailing into his chest. She caught the warm scent of his male skin as she was pressed to his length by his huge arms. The man swung her off her feet and away from the battle with Zeva.

Dylan and Jett both burst into her mind as she felt their tempers explode. A second later she was free as Ravid released her. She'd barely opened her eyes before Jett lifted her body and placed it behind his own. Another warrior appeared beside Ravid as Dylan and Jett faced off with him.

"Explain your actions, Ravid!"

Ravid stuck his finger out at Jett. "Your sister is a hellion and needs to be brought to heel."

"If you haven't touched her mind then it isn't your place." Jett struck the finger aside as he edged closer to the man. His body was tight with anger and he watched for any excuse to fight with the other warrior. The warrior next to Ravid pushed his companion back as he blocked Jett's next push. "Keenan..." The name was growled by Ravid but Keenan stayed in his path.

"Your sister runs before we are able to try, Jett. Now she takes refuge in the women's hall. Best you take up your anger with your mother. We would be most appreciative would your mother order her daughter to face us."

Ravid grunted but nodded his head. Dylan suddenly turned to consider Jessica. "Why did Ravid embrace you?"

He softened his voice but the words were still razor-sharp. She didn't like the accusation sitting in those dark eyes. The idea that Dylan even suspected she might have been unfaithful hurt.

Jett suddenly turned and stroked her face. Both men moved through her mind and every emotion became shared between them.

She shouldn't be so relieved to have Jett looking at her with a slightly guilty face. Shaking her head, she backed away from them both. "It beat hitting the dirt."

Jessica forced her eyes to look at the two warriors facing off with her...the word mates almost took hold in her mind. She shook her head and considered Ravid and Keenan. Both were hunks. The kind women slobbered over.

They did nothing for her. No tingle moving down her spine. No heat rushing along her veins. Her nipples were flat and completely uninterested. Nothing.

Except feeling hurt that Dylan and Jett might think her loose. She looked into Jett's eyes. It took only one solid glance from his face to send her blood pounding through her body. Heat rose as her breasts tightened and swelled. The side of her face burned from the simple touch of his fingers.

Dylan's eyes narrowed to slits as he stepped closer to touch her opposite cheek. The flesh burned as her passage flooded for him...for them.

It was too acute. Heat and need clawed away at her body as she caught the strong male scent from their bodies. But it was the desire for both of them that shook her body.

"Think whatever you like. I don't need the grief."

They grunted and she felt like screaming. Both men caged her with their bodies making it impossible to turn and storm away. Dylan caught her chin in an iron grip.

"I did not think you were the one at blame. Do not fault me for my concern. If your body were nothing but a release for mine, I would not care whose embrace you shared."

That made her feel cherished. A wave of warmth hit her as Jett firmly turned her to look into his eyes.

Dylan wasn't enough. The union they'd shared just last night seemed so incomplete as she stood there with both their hands touching her. Her body rejoiced as she caught the different scents of each of their bodies. They seemed to combine into something too powerful to resist.

Denying it was useless. She wouldn't just be lying to herself. Her body wasn't interested in any reason anyway. Her breasts were screaming for a touch, the nipples begging to be suckled.

Jett's hand slid down her neck as she arched it to allow his fingers to touch every last bit of her skin. Pleasure spiked towards her center as he lowered that hand until it firmly cupped her breast. Dylan moved behind her as his body gently moved hers closer to Jett's.

Captured between them, she felt so content. Jessica couldn't think beyond the scent of her warriors. The heat from their bodies wrapped her in an inferno that made her loathe the clothing that prevented their skin from connecting.

Jett groaned as she moved against him. His cock seemed to be permanently swollen since she'd set foot onto Alcandar. The scent of her arousal fired his blood making it impossible to resist the urge to touch. He caught the back of her head and tilted it up to his. Her lips parted as he demanded a deeper taste.

The sound of feet on the courtyard stones brought Jett to his senses. He raised his eyes to catch his brother's glittering ones. Hunger became a raw force that flowed freely between the three of them. Jett scooped Jessica off her feet as he turned towards the stairs that would lead them to their chamber.

Jett wasn't staying away from it for another second.

The buttons on her jacket popped as they went flying. Jessica gasped as Jett tossed the garment across the room. His eyes glittered with possession as he looked at her bare breasts.

"I dreamed of touching these last night." His hands cupped both her breasts as he bent to capture a nipple between his lips. Heat burned across her body as her passage suddenly flooded. His tongue worried the tight button of her nipple as two warm hands slid up her back.

Dylan caught the small lobe of her ear with his mouth. His hands gently smoothed the bare skin of her back as Jett licked her nipple one final time. Jett stepped back as Dylan continued to nip the smooth column of her neck. His eyes captured hers as he jerked his clothing off.

His body was magnificent. Dark hair covered his chest and the tightly corded muscles tempted her to touch them. His waist was tight and narrow. His cock stood at stiff attention as she looked over its length. The walls of her passage screamed for the hard thrust of that staff.

Her hand reached for him. Jessica curled her fingers around his length even as she sent her other hand behind her to tangle in Dylan's hair.

"Aye, *renina*, stroke me."

Her fingers traveled his length as she looked at the rounded head of that cock. She wanted more than the touch of her hand. She needed to ease the raging hunger that she felt pulsing from his mind. She was acutely aware of the frustration Jett had taken to bed last night as she was pleasured so well by Dylan.

"Go on, *heloni*, show him that delightful tongue of yours."

Dylan released her neck as he gently pushed her towards Jett. She dropped to her knees as she took his stiff cock in both her hands. She licked the head of his staff and listened to his male groan of pleasure. The sound encouraged her, making boldness spring up inside her as she felt her own power.

These men wanted her. She was an obsession to them and the only rule that mattered was the law of nature. She was their mate. It was time to indulge in the pure bliss of their union.

Her ears registered the sounds of Dylan's clothing hitting the floor. Jessica almost purred as she took a slow moment to circle the tip of Jett's cock with her tongue. Her blood pulsed with excitement as he gripped her hair between taut fingers. She lapped the length of his cock before covering the swollen head with her mouth.

His deep groan empowered her to be bolder. Both men were focused on her and she eagerly embraced the challenge of sating their combined appetites.

"Enough!" Jett pulled her head from his cock as he looked into her face. Her eyes sparkled with mischief as her fingers slipped down his length again. "Nay, *renina*, I will not be unmanned so quickly."

Jett bent and lifted her from the floor. The bed soon caught her body as he lay her on their bed. Lifting her eyes, Jessica watched as Dylan stretched his nude body across one side of the huge, round mattress. Hunger burned in his eyes as his hand firmly cupped one of her breasts. His head leaned forward, her nipple disappearing between his lips.

Her body twisted as hunger grew beyond the bounds of her reason. She didn't need to think, only to feel. Their hands were strong as they stroked her skin. Jett's body pushed her legs apart as he sent his fingers along the sensitive folds that covered her passage.

One finger parted the slick folds before finding the small bud at the top. Her cry filled the room as pleasure twisted under that single digit until her hips lifted, begging for a firmer touch. Demanding release from the pounding need clawing through her passage.

"Open your eyes, *renina*." Jett's voice was harsh with his own need. His finger froze as her hips twisted and strained to find release. Jessica opened her eyes as his opposite hand caught her hip and held her in place.

She was stunning. Jett filled his lungs with the hot scent of his female. Her bare skin gleamed and beckoned to him. Her woman's passage lay listening with her juices as she yielded her body to his touch.

It wasn't enough.

"Will you bind with me?"

Jessica almost screamed. Frustration ate at her body as she looked into the hard eyes of both men. She could smell their skin, taste the salty drops that she'd drawn from Jett's cock. His finger refused to move as the knot of tension in her belly became painful.

Sexual need couldn't be so strong! But her body denied the logic her brain tried to impose. She needed the release her spoken words could earn her. Her body demanded that surrender.

Instead she screamed as she flipped her body off the bed. Her knees hit the stone floor and the pain streaked through her passion-drugged system.

"I will not promise you that like this!"

Anger exploded in her head but it wasn't her temper. Both men were enraged as she stood and moved away from the bed that promised her so much pleasure. Instead, Jessica forced her legs to carry her body away from the two men who could relieve her aches.

"You make no sense!" Jett's jaw was clenched as he rose slowly from the bed. Jessica stepped back as he stepped towards her. His cock stuck out from his body with clear intention as his eyes assessed her position and the best method of capturing her.

"What's the problem, Jett? Afraid I won't make a lifelong commitment of my own free will?"

Dylan snorted and left the bed. "You are speaking nonsense, Jessica. We are mates, the evidence is slick on your thighs."

Jett lifted his hand and deliberately sniffed his fingers. His eyes closed to slits as his engorged cock twitched and jerked with hard arousal.

"I have to be more than your bed partner." Her own body was yearning for surrender but her will refused to relinquish her personality.

"Alcandian life is full of many things, Jessica. There are no chains in this chamber." Jett stepped closer as his mind caught the warring emotions inside her head.

"Then what's the rush, guys?"

Both men snorted. Hunger blazed through her mind as Jett closed another step closer to her.

"I will not spend another night alone, Jessica! Best you understand, I will have you and you will scream while I bring you to your pleasure."

Her body eagerly embraced his words. Jett felt the response as his body snapped and jumped forward. He caught her in an embrace that lifted her from the floor. His mouth captured hers as he moved until the wall pressed against her back.

His tongue thrust deeply into her mouth as Jett moved his hips between her thighs. His arms lifted her higher as his mouth took the deepest taste. Her lips clung to his as her body ignited into the flame of need that refused to wait. Her thighs parted to embrace the hard hips, the folds of her body opening as the hard head of his cock probed for entry.

"That is not the part I'm arguing with Jett. I do want you."

"Both?"

"Yes, both!"

His thrust was hard. Pure rapture exploded inside her passage as he filled the yearning emptiness inside her. His tongue thrust into her mouth as his hips pulled his length from her and sent it back into her body. Hard and deep, his thrusts drew a cry from her as the pleasure became too deep to contain.

"Tell me to stop, *renina*." His hips thrust forward on a hard stroke. "Tell me your cries are not ones of pleasure." His cock split her deeply as he pulled back and rammed forward again. "Deny that your body was made for me."

She couldn't. A sob escaped her as she felt the tension knotting around the length of his cock. His hips sent it into her body again and again as Dylan reached and stroked her mind.

Her eyes flew open to look over Jett's shoulder. He thrust again as she found Dylan watching them with a face that promised her more. More pleasure from the solid length of his own cock. His hand firmly stroked the swollen rod as he watched Jett thrust into her twisting body.

"Tell me what you want!" His hips didn't thrust fast enough! Jessica sent her own towards his as his hands controlled the speed. Refusing to grant her the final release.

"Please, Jett! I can't stand it!"

He granted her plea immediately. His hips doubled their speed as her body split with climax. It traveled through her skin until she screamed with the rapture. His body jerked between her thighs as his swollen cock thrust as deep as possible before the hot splash of his seed hit her core.

Her mind refused to work. Jessica floated on a wave of pleasure as her body rejoiced in the release. The bed welcomed her with its soft surface as the solid length of her lover filled her body once more.

Her eyes flew open to merge with Dylan's. "Deny me if you can, *heloni*." His body moved with powerful strokes as her belly responded with renewed hunger. Instead of speeding and twisting, the need grew in a steady tension that centered around his cock. Her hips lifted for the hard thrust as her belly demanded another release from the ache within her.

Dylan groaned as the walls of her passage gripped his cock. She lifted beneath him as her mind relinquished its battle against their union. Jett stroked her breast as Dylan listened to the delicate cries coming from her throat. His body demanded the ultimate release but he gritted his teeth to contain the climax.

His mate's pleasure would come first.

Hard and hot, her need refused to stop growing. Jessica gasped and panted as her hips frantically lifted for Dylan. Her passage ached for the thrust of his hard flesh. Her thighs spread even wider as she tried to gain even deeper penetration. Her hand reached for the second cock she craved. Jett groaned as she stroked his length and turned her head to capture the head between her lips.

Pleasure flowed between them all. It centered under Dylan's hard thrust and coursed through her body to the hard cock between her lips. Her hips lifted as she took more of Jett's cock between her lips and felt his fingers twist into her hair.

She shattered once again as Dylan gasped and ground his length deep inside her body. Hot seed filled her belly as the pleasure contracted around her womb. Tears pricked her eyelids as she felt the wave of pleasure course through her flesh. Nothing stopped it, no reason or logic. Jett's hand dug into her head as his cock exploded in her mouth. His seed hit her tongue as she pulled every last drop from him.

Heavy breathing was the only sound that filled the chamber. Four hands smoothed and caressed her body and it just felt right.

Jett scooped her off the bed and walked towards the bathing pool. The water rose around her skin as Dylan rolled off the bed and came to join them. Jessica suddenly understood why the pool was so large.

It was made for three.

Dylan reached for the soap and began to slip it along her shoulders. It seemed so natural to let him bathe her. All Jessica felt was the need to begin applying the soap to his broad chest in return.

"Why do I displease you?" Jett's voice was rough with anger.

"It's not you."

"Then explain." This time Dylan's voice issued the command. Jessica considered the two magnificent males before letting her mind recall just why she shouldn't have them both.

"A woman who has multiple lovers is considered immoral on my world."

A harsh grunt from Dylan was her reply. Jett stepped closer and began to join Dylan's efforts to bathe her. His hands slipped over the globes of her breasts bringing the sensitive mounds to tingling awareness.

"Yet there are men who have multiple mates on your world and that is considered a legal union."

"Well, yes, in some religions that is true." Jessica found her hands applying soap to one hard set of pectoral muscles before she turned to attend to another set. Both men continued to bathe her as if it were the most natural of practices.

"Your species is coded to produce too many females. It is logical that many women must accept a union that includes another woman or remain celibate and childless."

Jessica felt her mind trying to grasp that logic. It sounded far too reasonable for the teachings of a lifetime that told her monogamy was the only moral union. But Jett had a point. There were several religions that allowed multiple wives. If you took a moment to consider the fact that Alcandians were the opposite of humans...that left her mind with plenty of reason to embrace that her having two husbands might be as common as multiple wives back on Earth.

"Those women don't marry the same man at the same time."

"Humans can still physically mate with the wrong partner. The union will not be a binding one. Your rising abandonment rates prove that." Jett lifted her chin as he finished his statement. His eyes cut into her as she caught the unmistakable trace of hurt in his emotions. He believed she was choosing Dylan over him. But the truth was, she couldn't make a choice between them.

But she would have to make one choice soon. Bind or offer her body to some of the warriors below. Her skin shrank as she considered letting Keenan or Ravid touch her. A shudder shook her frame as she felt the smooth slide of Dylan's and Jett's hands across her body. The difference was stark. Here she was their treasured mate. Pleasure flowed from the contact as she felt the security of their need for her in return.

*Bloody hell…* What was she going to do now?

\* \* \* \* \*

Lanai showed up at the crack of dawn once more. This time the woman was humming as she opened the curtains.

"I was born on Earth, you know. Long before there were rules to bindings. My mates abducted me but they valued my heart highly enough to offer me freedom."

She hadn't known that. Jessica looked at Lanai as Dylan's mother shook out another new robe for her to wear. It was deep burgundy. The fabric obviously expensive and woven with skill.

"I struggled with my decision just as you are now. Two men—my father would have taken his belt to me if he'd known." Lanai turned and looked at Jessica with an expression of understanding instead of the bright smile the woman had been treating her to. "I have never regretted my choice."

"But Jessica, many Alcandian brides come from cultures that would view our unions as immoral. Many Earth brides face the unknown, even cross oceans to marry men they have only met between the pages of a letter. You have to trust your feelings. Everything else will find its way. The only true thing you have in life is love."

"I don't love Dylan and Jett."

"Don't you?" Lanai's eyes were far too knowing as they inspected her face. "You have lain with them now. Admit you have never felt the sheer volume of pleasure before in your life. Why were you a virgin, Jessica?"

"For good reason! I wanted to make sure I was making a good choice..."

"Hush, child!" Lanai's voice cracked with every year of her wisdom. "You never felt so much need twisting inside you before. Do they still sing songs about love at first sight? I wonder, what did my son make you feel the first time his eyes met yours?"

Jessica remembered Dylan in her kitchen like it had happened just two minutes ago. Her nipples even beaded as she thought about the surge of heat he had always ignited in her.

"Would it have been so different if he'd meet you at some bar? Men and women meet in so many different ways. Don't try to determine which ones are the right ones. It is nature's way. The genders are drawn to each other, only here we are only truly affected by our mates. It's so much more intense."

"Yeah, everyone keeps telling me this is the one or two for me."

Lanai laughed and smiled at Jessica. "Youth is wasted on the young, my dear child. When you get to my age, you learn to take life by the seat of your pants. It's a much better ride that way."

Jessica laughed. Wasn't that just the way she had always looked at her own life? To hell with the rules! She was going to live like tomorrow was the end.

"I get your point, Lanai, and I promise you I will think about it."

"I told you my son had made no mistake. You are made of strong enough mettle to love both your mates."

Lanai left on silent feet. The curtain swished closed as Jessica looked at the burgundy robe. It was suspended in midair by some unseen force. Lying on the tile floor was her business suit. Her bra was on top of the linen jacket as her high-heeled shoes lay next to it.

Jessica looked at the burgundy robe again as she noticed the difference in it. The robe was made to clothe her body just as it was. The Alcandians didn't try to change the female to suit some image. Back on Earth there was always the hottest new trend. This year curves, next season slim. The soft moccasin boots on her feet were made to walk in. Not contort her feet into some fashionable shape while pushing her bottom into the air. Instead the Alcandian clothing was made to suit life.

She bent and hooked the strap of her bra with one finger. She looked at the lace and elastic garment as her breasts actually protested her strapping them into the thing again.

Alcandar was certainly a comfortable world in many ways. So why did they have to ruin the effect with kidnapping? The memory of Dylan standing in her kitchen popped into her mind. He had asked.

So, because she'd turned him down the man had just decided to claim her? That was barbaric. Jessica waited but her temper never arrived. Instead she was left with the glaring truth that if Dylan had walked away, she never would have shared the last few hours with him and Jett.

Even now, her body seemed to almost glow with the aftereffect of the pleasure she'd found between their bodies.

The burgundy robe beckoned to her. All she had to do was slip into the garment and walk down those stairs tonight. Two men were waiting to publicly promise her their allegiance.

Her body responded to that idea. Her skin almost crawled as she thought about Bryan's kiss. She'd spent so much time attempting to cultivate passion for the man. Dylan and Jett ignited passion within her.

Too many things made too much sense. Jessica turned towards the curtain and left the chamber. The remaining sunlight seemed to be ticking away her opportunities. Her brain spun with the importance of her decision.

# Chapter Eight

**ဢ**

The waterfalls didn't look any different but the serenity she'd found there wasn't present today. Jessica stood and looked at them with eyes that only wanted to see Jett standing there with her.

"Your pardon, *darmasha*, but I would make my presence known to you."

Jessica turned to find Keenan lounging in one of the trees. The huge man was expertly perched along a thick branch, his tightly corded legs used to keep his body from falling towards the ground. He granted her a boyish smile as she traced his body with her eyes.

She hadn't expected the smile from this warrior. He was every inch a mature man. Tightly leashed strength all combined into the very definition of male. Nothing stirred in her. She even slid her eyes to the bulge in his pants and still her breasts didn't swell, the nipples didn't rise. All she could think was that some woman would be lucky to have the warrior.

"I see it is true." Keenan considered her with sharp eyes before he jumped to the ground and landed on steady feet. He rose to his full height and moved towards her.

"What's true?"

"You are resisting the binding."

"That's none of your business. And I call it contemplating."

That smile appeared again, only this time it was much more mature. The man was amused by her.

"You are here and not preparing for your ceremony."

His superior attitude rubbed her pride. "It doesn't take that long to put on a jacket." Or to take it off either. Her breasts did tingle as she considered the fact that Jett and Dylan would happily take that burgundy coat off her tonight once she'd pledged herself to them.

Temptation set up a cruel pounding in her blood that made its way through her circulatory system.

"Ah, then you are not here to offer yourself to me so that Dylan and Jett will reject you? I am lonely, as you humans like to say."

Her eyes rounded with horror as she barely controlled the need to gag. The physical response was so strong, all Jessica managed to do was keep her jaw shut. Keenan's eyes didn't miss the pallor of her face as she struggled against the tide of revulsion his offer produced.

He threw his head back and laughed.

"Forgive me, *darmasha*! I have been in need of amusement all day. A warrior does not take the rejection of his mate well. Zeva soured my temper well and truly this morning."

"Zeva told me she wasn't bound."

Keenan sobered as his eyes grew somber and his face reflected resignation.

"Aye, it is with great regret that I confess, I have not been able to force her to face me or my brother."

The warrior's frustration was carried through his voice. "How can she hide from you?"

"Maidens do not mingle with warriors. The women's sections are off-limits to unbound warriors such as me. Once a warrior touches his mate the blood burns with a fever for her. If she is too tender of years, it can drive him insane while he waits for her to reach her eighteenth year."

"So, how do you know Zeva is your mate?"

Keenan shook his head as he leaned against the trunk of a tree. "I do not, yet I am drawn to her. The need to touch her mind burns in my every thought. She resists." His eyes suddenly burned with solid intent as he considered her.

"Why do you resist binding? I would try to understand this reaction of a female."

"I…well…I don't know Dylan and Jett that well." Keenan lifted one dark eyebrow. Her cheeks flooded with heat as she chose that moment to recall the half wall in their chamber.

"I just need more time."

Keenan grunted. He pushed away from the tree and strode towards her. His hand cupped her chin as his eyes probed hers. No spark crossed the ebony depths of his eyes. Her breath stayed even and slow. Attraction didn't seem to rise in either one of them, not even the cheap lust that she'd witnessed in Bryan's face while Gwen had been catering to his sexual fantasies.

"Then ask for it."

Her chin was free as the large man turned to leave. "You mean, this doesn't have to happen tonight?"

"We are warriors, *darmasha*, not barbarians. A mate's needs touch us deeply." He turned to point a single finger at her. "But we do not play boy's games. If all you want is some spineless boy who will jump to your whims, go back to Earth."

\* \* \* \* \*

*Go back to Earth.*

Those words bounced around in her head as they seemed to imply it was time to grow up. Jessica turned and looked at the path that would lead her back to Dylan and Jett.

She set off on it not knowing what she sought. Only that the answer lay with the three of them. The door panel of the main house shimmered as she touched it.

The hall was filling with warriors as the sun began to set. Jett paced the length of one of the walkways as Dylan straddled a bench and looked at the other man with a brooding expression. Conversation was hushed tonight. Eyes lit onto her the second she crossed into the hall.

Jessica didn't care. She needed to know. Was that flame of attraction still as brilliant now that she'd surrendered her body completely to them? Would her hunger be the same now that she'd tasted the forbidden fruit of a ménage? Had she just needed the taste of forbidden fruit?

Jessica intended to find out.

She held her head high as she crossed the hall. It really didn't matter who watched her. It was her body and her choice. Dylan raised his eyes and the spark of electricity zipped across the distance making her tingle.

Jett immediately jerked around. A shiver ran right down to her toes as she watched both pairs of eyes study her approach. The uncertainty coming from their minds bothered her. Keenan's words were lodged in her memory. These were indeed men. She wanted the hard bodies of these warriors and with that came the price of not stomping on their pride.

"I would like one more day, before our binding ceremony."

Neither man had expected the request. Jett sent Dylan a hard look before he inclined his head towards her. "If you like, *renina*."

"This would make you more comfortable?" Dylan didn't rise from his seat. Instead his knuckles were white as he gripped his drinking cup. Emotion was thick between their minds. Need, frustration, it all mingled as uncertainty rose to the top of it all.

"I don't know, but I want the chance to find out."

"Then it is yours, *heloni*."

His voice sounded as disappointed as Jett's had. Jessica suddenly smiled as she discovered the power of asking. It certainly hadn't been all that difficult. She turned and walked back towards their chamber. Disappointment flared inside her mind making her stop.

She turned to see Jett joining Dylan at the table. Dylan passed his brother a drinking cup as the two men lifted them in unison.

A silly smile covered her face as she looked at the clear proof of their willingness to please her. She could feel the need pulsing from their bodies as her own mirrored it. Yet they resisted it in the face of what they believed to be her need to think.

"Well, I'm not going to find much out if you two are going to stay down here all night. I'll be upstairs when you finish those drinks."

Jessica turned as the hall filled with the heavy, approving sound of male amusement. Drinking cups were raised to her as she made her way towards the stairs.

She didn't care if every man there did know she was going upstairs to have wild sex with two men.

The only thing that mattered was if Jett and Dylan wanted to be those two men.

\* \* \* \* \*

She had to be a little crazy. The burgundy robe greeted Jessica as she made her way into the sleeping chamber. She looked around the room like it was the first time she'd really seen it.

Everything in it made for three people. On Earth everything was marketed for couples. Furniture, houses, beds, it was so natural to believe that was the only way nature intended it to be.

Alcandar held a different view. Right below her were men who didn't think a harsh thought about her going to bed with two men. Words like whore or hussy hadn't been muttered as she'd calmly informed Dylan and Jett that she would be waiting upstairs for them.

Hell, even her own brother didn't take offense.

At the moment, Jessica wasn't sure she was even worried about it anymore. How could she think about society's rules when her blood was accelerating at the mere idea that that curtain might move aside any second to admit two men whose sole purpose was to spend the night with her on that made for three bed?

Tilting her head, Jessica watched that fabric. Her breath was lodged in her throat as she waited for it to shift. Loneliness seemed to surround her in the empty room. It didn't bring her relief to be in the vast stone chamber alone. Instead all she noticed was the absence of her warriors.

Maybe they wouldn't come.

Her body shrieked at the idea of Jett and Dylan choosing their male buddies over her.

The curtain was sent towards the wall with a swift blow. The fabric bounced and shook as Dylan moved into the chamber, Jett was a half step from his back. They stood for a moment to regard her. Both faces turned to masks of stone as they refused to expose their feeling to her uncertain mood.

Jett looked at the burgundy robe and grinned. He slapped Dylan on the shoulder before moving towards the robe. "My mother won."

"This time." Dylan growled the words but his face lacked any true animosity. Jett inspected the binding robe before turning his half-grin onto Jessica.

"Paneil adores *Transhi* stones. Lanai prefers *Keniya*. They are much lighter in color."

"Lanai is blonde, darker shades aren't her best ones."

Jett's fingers lifted a lock of her hair from her shoulder and considered it a moment. "The *Transhi* robe will suit you well."

His face had softened, making her stare at him in wonder. The stiff exterior of the warrior was giving way to the face of a lover. "Do your mothers disagree often?"

Male amusement filled the chamber. Dylan's hands suddenly appeared and stroked the length of her arms. Her body responded immediately to the touch. Pleasure slipped along her skin as he moved his hands back to her shoulders and firmly smoothed his palms down her limbs once more.

"When you swell with child they will become unbearable to live with."

"Oh..." She hadn't thought about pregnancy. Jessica considered her flat tummy and the very real idea that inside her could already be a tiny growth that would mature into a baby.

"Wouldn't only one of them be excited about a baby?"

Jett's hand caught her chin and raised her eyes to his. "Nay, you are our mate. Any child of your body will be claimed by both of us."

Dylan's hands moved back up her body until they found the two buttons that held her coat closed. His hard body brushed along the length of her back as he undid the garment. Jett's eyes turned hard as he dropped his gaze to her lips. Hunger shone from those eyes as Dylan spread the edges of her coat open and over her shoulders.

She wanted his kiss so badly. Dylan's hands cupped the bare globes of her breasts as pleasure shot along her nerves. Jett traced the fullness of her lower lip with his thumb as Dylan caught her nipples with his fingers.

"Kiss me."

Her mouth was dry as she tried to focus on Jett's command. The sharp tug and pull on her nipples made it hard to do anything but experience the pure brilliance of sensation that the two male bodies surrounding her produced.

"Come here and kiss me."

Jett wouldn't relent either. Jessica fought for enough brainpower to do as he asked. She licked her lips as she tried to reach for his neck. Her fingers shook as she found the heat from his large body radiating through the coat he wore. She frowned at the fabric and reached for one of the buttons that held it closed. Deep male amusement surrounded her as Jett helped send this clothing towards the floor. Dylan mirrored his actions as Jessica slid her fingers through Jett's chest hair.

Her nose caught the heavy scent of his skin as she stretched onto her toes for the taste of his mouth. She needed it desperately in that moment. Her breasts were free and begging for more from Dylan's hands.

It was the sweetest torment waiting for her kiss. Jett felt the prickle of sensation as it bordered on pain. Her soft mouth trembled as she reached for him. Delicate hands slipped up his chest as she tried to obey his order.

He needed her to reach for him. Show him the desire he felt blazing through her mind. Prove that she wasn't complete without them. Her lips caught his as they trembled. Dylan lifted her body into Jett's embrace as Jett caught her mouth with his and sent his tongue thrusting deeply between her lips. Her tongue found his as he stroked the length of hers.

His cock stiffened as her body melted against his. He had been raging for her since the moment he'd parted company with her. The scent of hot arousal mixed inside his head with the pulsing throb of his staff. The need to mate was strong, the desire to spread her thighs and look at the wet flow from her body almost overwhelming.

A little moan escaped her throat as Dylan stripped her last garment. He didn't rise from the floor but smoothed his hands over her legs. Every part of her was so intensely female. He stopped on the top of one thigh as Jett released her lips. Her eyes glistened with desire as she looked at him.

"What is it you want to discover, *heloni*?" Dylan moved his hand until it covered the bare mons of her sex. A shiver traveled down her body making him grin.

He pushed to his feet, but his hand stayed right over her mons. Jessica felt her breath freeze as she looked into Jett's demanding eyes. He didn't move. Instead Jett captured her nipples and pinched them with a force that stopped just short of pain. The sharp sensation traveled straight into her core as her hips twitched towards the hand covering the little bud that was demanding more attention.

Suddenly, she was immensely grateful for the hair removal. Dylan's fingers glided easily over her bare sex and not even a hair interfered in the sensation.

"What do you want?" It was a husky whisper of temptation. One finger gently parted her folds but only the barest amount. It left and returned but not any deeper. Her body shook as it anticipated that contact.

"Touch me." God, just touch her! The need screamed through her as his finger split her folds but stopped short again.

"Hmm..." The deep sound rumbled out of Jett. His hands suddenly cupped the twin cheeks of her bottom. Dylan's finger re-parted her folds and penetrated until it gently touched the hard nub at the top of her sex. The two hands on her bottom lifted and squeezed as Dylan's finger began to gently rub the aching nub.

She cried as pleasure shot up into her belly. Fluid eased down the walls of her passage as Dylan pressed the hard length of his staff against her bottom. Wicked ideas formed in her mind as the possibilities of both men pleasuring her hit. They could keep her body filled with hard male flesh for endless time. Trading off as Zeva had said.

"Shall we make you cry loud enough for every warrior below to hear?" Her head jerked around to look at Dylan as his finger began to move faster. Pleasure battled with horror as she considered the determination glittering in his eyes. Jett turned her to face Dylan as he smoothed his hands over her bottom again.

"It would please me well to know they would hear you screaming for me."

"Whose name will you cry out first?" The head of Jett's cock nudged her as he parted the cheeks of her bottom. His hard flesh slipped between her thighs where her juices had flowed past the opening to her body. Her belly clenched as the hard head probed the aching entrance.

"You have not answered my brother, *renina.*" Jett stopped short of the penetration she craved. Instead he lingered with just the hard touch of his staff to her sex. His hands settled onto her hips as she lifted her bottom for his possession. His teeth nipped her ear as his cock stayed exactly in place and his hand held her hips firmly.

"Shall I decide how to touch you? You have refused to honor me. Are you certain you want to risk the chastisement I might decide you deserve?" His hand rubbed one side of her bottom making her eyes fly open with shock. Surely he wouldn't...punish her. Would he?

A solid smack landed on her bottom making her yelp. Dylan clasped her arms and held her in place as Jett rubbed the spot.

"I haven't been spanked since I was a child!"

Jett thrust his cock into her body in one swift thrust. Her body screamed with pleasure.

Jett grunted. "You are no child now. Yet, I confess to enjoying treating you like one."

"You can't spank me!" He hadn't moved that hard length lodged inside her. Her passage gripped and clutched at it as she tried to move her hips. Both men held her exactly in place. Sweat beaded on her skin as the need became desperate.

"You are so certain what cannot be done, my *renina.* Maybe we should discuss what can be done to make you yield. To make you scream."

Another smack landed on her bottom. Jett's hips pulled and thrust deeply into her. A cry caught in her throat as he penetrated her aching depths. His hand landed on her bottom again making the sensation double. The small smacking pain mingled with the deep thrust of his cock making her moan deep and long. Her bottom pushed towards the attention.

It wasn't enough. She hung on the border of climax as she pushed back towards her lover. She needed more!

"What do you need, *heloni*?" Dylan wasn't asking. He demanded with a rough voice as another blow landed on her bottom. Her eyes flew open to find him watching her face. Her body screamed as Jett thrust and withdrew but it never reached the little nub of her pleasure at the top of her sex.

"Touch me, Dylan, please."

His hand cupped her mons as she tried to decide which way to move her hips. She was caught between them both, needing them together to ease the screaming desire inside her body. Her feet left the floor as she wrapped her arms around Dylan's shoulders and Jett's hand held her weight by her hips.

"Oh yes…please…harder."

Everything drew into a knot that twisted and tightened under their combined efforts. Her body simply responded and theirs catered to her needs. Dylan stopped just short of the speed she craved. Frustration made her cry as Jett let another spank land on her cheek.

"Dylan!"

Her voice bounced off the walls of the chamber but he responded immediately. Jett thrust as Dylan let his finger apply the right pressure and she shattered as pleasure made her moan low and deep. The heavy pound of Jett's heart hit her ears as his body jerked and thrust. His cock erupted inside her body as his arm captured her waist and held her in place.

Dylan caught her face and lowered his mouth to hers as pleasure rippled through her. Jett lifted her from his cock and held her bottom up as Dylan's cock probed for entry. Her thighs eagerly parted as he thrust forward and Jett pressed her towards the penetration.

Jessica clung to Dylan's chest and Jett pressed against her back. Dylan thrust into her body on hard strokes that made her moan. Once again pleasure flowed between them like a current, making it impossible to separate whose body felt what. The hard cock inside her jerked and thrust as her passage gripped and milked it. Hot seed jutted into her body as two sets of arms embraced her.

\* \* \* \* \*

The soft surface of the bed hit her back as Jessica let her eyes flutter open. The splash of water hit her ears and she looked at Jett as he entered the sunken pool. Water glistened off his chest and the sculpted perfection of his arms.

"I think it is time I told you what I want, *heloni*." She shivered. Dylan grinned and traced the gooseflesh that covered her arm. So delicate and soft. Her skin amazed him. Coupled with the scent from her climax, control seemed to slip through his grasp. The need to bury his length between her thighs grew until his mind couldn't seem to hold another idea. Only her spread beneath him as his cock penetrated and drove into her core.

What he wanted? Jessica licked her lips and watched his eyes home in on the motion. Her body still floated on the wave of pleasure yet hungered for so much more. It was like she'd been starving for years and only now found the nourishment her body craved.

His swollen cock stood away from his body. Reaching up, Jessica grasped it in her hand. She suddenly wanted to be the one enticing the responses. Rolling over she lay on her side and stroked the length of his member.

"Well…I would be interested in discovering what you want." Her bottom still smarted but the little pulses of pleasure traveled straight into her passage where it triggered another acute need to be filled. In her hand lay the flesh she wanted to end that need.

But first, she was going to listen to him moan. She didn't wait but stretched forward until her tongue made a lazy circle around the head of his cock. The swift intake of breath touched her ears making her bold.

Dylan caught her head as her mouth took his cock. It was the sweetest of torments. Hot and wet, she sucked and pulled at the flesh that begged him for release. Instead he ground his teeth and let her lick the rounded head before pulling half of it into her mouth. Her little hands cupped the twin sacs beneath his cock making him groan.

She laughed around his member as her tongue returned to its teasing. The need to bind her to him raged as his body proclaimed just how perfectly suited they were for each other. Release tried to conquer his control, but he wanted more than her mouth tonight.

His moan drove her insane. She liked the male rumble so much it almost scared her. Once again their minds mingled as she licked and pulled on his staff. Jett left the water, making her body quiver as she tried to guess where he might decide to touch her while her attention was centered on Dylan.

The bed moved as Jett joined them. His large body stretched out along hers. His hands smoothed over her hips before one of his knees pressed between her legs to separate them. The tip of his cock slipped easily between the folds of her sex as Dylan's fingers held her mouth in place.

The hard thrust from Jett's body made her cry as pleasure erupted from the penetration.

"You were made to take me, *heloni*." She believed him. Somehow, in her heart she knew it. Pleasure spiked as Dylan jerked and she closed her lips tightly around his cock. His face was drawn tight as control crumbled and pure male need surfaced.

Climax took him before hers crested. His staff jerked and emptied his seed into her mouth. Her fingers curled around his cock as she pulled and stroked him through the release.

Jett thrust harder into her body from behind as she continued to lick Dylan's cock. "Aye, *renina*, I will not leave you burning." Jett suddenly rolled over and took her with him. His wide shoulders hit the surface of the bed as Dylan lifted her to straddle Jett's lean hips. His brother's cock thrust up and Dylan lifted her into place above it.

"Lift your bottom and take me." Jett's voice was husky and hard. Bracing her knees of either side of his lean hips, she rose above her warrior and purred as the head of his cock nudged the opening of her body.

"Now down." She obeyed and gasped as his cock stretched her body to once again admit the deep penetration of a mate. The walls of her passage protested but the promise of pleasure was too much.

"Aye, now lean forward and brace your hands on my chest so that your breasts will hang towards me."

"You like giving orders don't you?" Her voice was thin as she struggled against the need to do exactly what Jett wanted immediately. Her hips rose and fell on his staff as she struggled to maintain some measure of self-awareness.

Jett smacked her bottom again. The sting made her yelp but her passage jerked and gripped the hard length of his sex too. The sensation was sharp but incredible. A smug smile lifted Jett's mouth as he watched her eyes intently.

"You enjoy hearing me say what I want from you out loud. I see it in your eyes, *renina*. There is no shame in pleasuring you." Another blow hit her bottom as Jett lifted his hips to buck under her. "And you like being spanked like a woman."

She moaned as climax threatened but didn't break over her twisting belly. Instead she hovered on the edge as her thighs tried to move her faster, closer to the edge of desire and satisfaction. Jett suddenly froze as his hips bucked and buried his cock deeply inside her.

"Tell me how much you like my hand on your sweet bottom."

She lifted and plunged down but it lacked the same hard spike of pleasure when Jett didn't move his hand from its resting place over the fading sensation of his last spank.

"Jett, please!!!"

"Please what, Jessica? There are so many things I could do."

His fingers found the fount of her sex and the swollen bud hidden there. His hips bucked as his chest let out a harsh grunt. He rubbed her little nub as he sent his cock deeply into her body. She cried as the pleasure spiked through her. Her throat couldn't contain the sound, it rose from the very pit of their joined bodies. But she needed more!

"Spank me."

A hand landed on her bottom as she rose off his hard length. Dylan nipped her ear as he leaned against her back. Jett's finger circled her swollen nub before she plunged down onto his cock again.

It was Dylan who smacked her bottom sending her into climax. They held her between their bodies as the world shattered around her. Tossing and jerking her body until only pleasure registered in her mind.

Dylan scooped her body off the bed the second Jett rolled over. A low grumble came from Jett as Dylan separated them.

"Now who is greedy, brother?"

Jessica opened her eyes in horror as she contemplated the idea that Dylan might want even more from her. Her muscles were limp from the excessive stimulation. Fatigue was trying to claim her as she sent her fingers through the dense mat of hair covering Dylan's chest.

He took her across the chamber to the sunken bathing pool. He stepped right down into it with her still cradled in his embrace. The smell of his warm male skin made her sigh as he released her legs and let them lower into the warm water.

Her muscles rejoiced. Her throat hummed with pleasure as she pushed against his chest. His arms released her and she sank down into the inviting warmth of the pool.

Dylan watched her. His chest felt too tight as he followed her with his eyes. Warriors shouldn't have such deep emotions, yet his mate seemed to have found them.

Jessica felt Dylan. He whispered through her mind with a touch full of tenderness. She looked up to find his lips turned up into the first boyish smile she'd ever seen on his lips. His body was so toned and drawn that it was easy to assume he was invincible. Something like tenderness wasn't what she expected from her warrior.

"Have you found your answers, *heloni*?" His voice was gruff as he tried to maintain his dignity. The idea touched her deeply. Here, inside this chamber, her needs took priority. That washed her in an emotion that felt like being cherished.

"I don't know." The truth was, she wasn't sure what her question had been. She certainly had made discoveries though. Never had she ever considered spanking erotic.

Jett grunted as he swung his legs over the rim of the pool. Both men watched her as their frustration invaded her thoughts.

"It's not just about sex to me. Marriage should be about more."

"You assume it would not be so." Dylan crossed his arms with his statement. For the first time Jessica noticed it was a defensive posture. One meant to protect his feelings from her rejection.

"Relationships take time to grow." Jett was trying to hold his frustration back as well. His fingers were curled over the lip of the pool. "Yet even on Earth couples take their pleasures during your so-called dates."

"True." In fact she'd kissed more than one guy on the first date.

"We are simply honest here. A warrior does not touch a female that he will not offer his protection to." Jett grunted approval at Dylan's words. Jessica found herself liking the sound of those words too.

"Well, it might help if you two took the time to talk to me." They both grunted and she rolled her eyes.

"You refused me, and I never return from the hunt empty-handed!" Dylan's eyes almost glowed. The black orbs flashed blue electricity at her as his lips curled back to display his teeth.

"Boys talk, men take action, Jessica. Best you understand that." Jett looked at her from behind the stone mask he often wore. The strength touched her on a deep, primitive level. Something inside her approved of their stance.

Her logical brain tried to tell her it was a caveman mentality but she still felt the rush of warmth as it spread across her skin. They weren't just sexy. They were superior mates and she'd be lying if she didn't admit to noticing that fact. The truth was, she admired it. It made her tingle and shiver in places that were just as primitive.

"I guess I do. But I'm not a pet. Maybe that's what you two are missing."

"Explain." Jett sounded like he was demanding but maybe that wasn't a bad thing. She couldn't expect them to understand her. They came from a different world, for heaven's sake.

"Everyone is rushing me towards a lifelong commitment. What's the hurry?"

Dylan's arm shot out at light speed to encircle her waist. He hauled her into contact with his body as the water swished out of the way. Suddenly she wasn't so tired anymore. The hard length of his body sent sensation shooting through hers until her passage awakened with a whimper.

Jett pressed against her back making her skin whine for more from them. Her nerve endings weren't overloaded anymore, instead they had learned to send the stimulation speeding through her system at an amazing rate. Her body melted and registered theirs as her hips found the length of Dylan's cock against her belly.

"This is our hurry, Jessica. Would you have me take your body and leave your bed without honoring you in front of other warriors?" Dylan was furious. Anger zipped right into her mind as he captured her mouth and pushed her lips open in surrender.

She welcomed that kiss as Jett gently bit her shoulder. Their hands seemed to encase her in their touches. Too many to separate and she didn't want to anyway. Instead there was only pleasure. Contentment followed so closely as they fed the hunger that was only for them.

\* \* \* \* \*

She woke to darkness. Jessica moved and shifted in the bed. Jett and Dylan slept on either side of her tonight. Jett's eyes opened in response to her movement. They glittered in the meager light before he tucked an arm around her waist and pulled her into contact with his warmth.

Dylan's eyes snapped open immediately as he looked for the reason she wasn't touching him any longer. He moved until her legs tangled with his and one hand rested on her bent thigh.

It seemed so natural. Her conscience wasn't keeping her awake with the spinning thoughts of her misbehavior. Instead she just wanted to absorb the comfort that surrounded her.

Contentment radiated from her. Sleep wasn't being held off by the endless worries of everyday life. Even the idea of pregnancy didn't bother her.

The warriors who held her would never be angry over a coming baby. She knew it in her heart. They would plaster those huge, smug grins on their faces and brag to their buddies.

Maybe it was time to stop worrying so much about details. Her heart hummed with contentment as her eyes fluttered shut. Just possibly, this was what love was.

\* \* \* \* \*

"Jessica? Get up."

Cole was almost whispering. He reached for her shoulder and shook it. He ripped the bedding aside and frowned as he took in her nudity.

Jessica jumped and sent herself over the opposite side. She grabbed a rumbled blanket and wrapped it around herself.

"Cole!"

"Quiet. Get dressed. I can to get you out of here, but we have to go now."

"I thought that was impossible."

Cole looked at her with solemn eyes. They reflected the pain of failure before he found her clothes and tossed them across the bed to her. He turned his back and waited.

"You're my sister." It was a flat statement. One she understood. Wasn't that one of the major reasons those goons hadn't had to drag her into that wormhole? She wouldn't refuse to help her brother out if he needed her.

"Come on, Jett is arguing with Ravid. We have to get out of here before he returns."

Cole grabbed her hand and jerked her towards the curtain. He used his hand to pull the fabric just barely away from the stone wall before tipping his head to look down the stairs.

He nodded before sweeping the fabric aside and pulling her down the steps. She struggled to keep up. Cole took the stairs at a frantic pace before ducking through the door panel. He immediately fell into a normal walking pace as they stepped into the sunshine.

"Smile and act like we are having some good sibling fun, Sis."

But they weren't having fun. Cole's body was tight with tension. Jessica felt her chest constricting as she left the house behind. Each step took her away from Dylan and Jett.

Her brain was shaking off sleep as they traveled back over the same steps that Dylan had carried her over so proudly. The courtyard came into sight as Cole pulled her right down into it and began crossing it. They drew a few greetings but nothing more. Everyone seemed to be going about their day. Cole nodded back and pulled her forward.

The wormhole was brilliant. The energy cracking and popping. There wasn't another soul in the building. That was another little detail that proclaimed how advanced the Alcandians were.

On Earth, they were standing vigil over the other end of the portal because her fellow humans were desperate to understand the thing. They recorded every detail in their quest to become more knowledgeable.

Dylan's words haunted her as she stared at the open gate. Conquer. Earth had bargained with the Alcandians in order to avoid being invaded. That sounded so harsh but it was still true.

"Jessica, what are you doing?" Zeva appeared at the doorway and frowned at her. The Alcandian female looked at a small monitor in her hand before she looked back around the room. "How long have you been here?"

The dark corners of the room came to life with her words. Men formed from the darkness as Zeva jumped into deadly form. Her assailants gave a few harsh grunts before they overwhelmed her ability to defend her body.

"Excellent work, Somerton."

"What in the hell are you doing here?" Cole's body went rigid with his furry. Zeva was dragged forward by black-clad men that peered at her through slits in their ski masks. If her brother wasn't so angry she could have laughed at the extreme-looking commando team. Instead she eased away from her brother but felt her skin tighten as hands appeared on her arms just as solidly as the ones on Zeva.

"Duty, Somerton, remember what that is? Well, today we take back Earth's security and kick these alien scumbags off our planet." A pair of eyes shifted from Cole to her and Jessica felt the heat of hatred hit her. His eyes raked over her before he gave a quick jerk of his head. "Thanks to your intelligence, Somerton, once we have a couple of their bitches, these Alcandians won't put up much fight. You found their soft spot."

Jessica was pulled towards the current and felt the hair on her head begin to rise. She could not come back. Earth intended to close the gateway and end all contact with Alcandar. "Let me go!"

Those hard eyes shot to her face as a sneer covered his mouth. "Shut up. If you like this kind of ménage à trois crap, I'm sure you can find a couple of dicks on your own world to scratch the itch."

The hold on her arms became brutal. Jessica was yanked towards the wormhole and shoved into its pulsing current. Cole's angry words hit her ears as her body was pulled through space and dumped back onto Earth.

"Let me go!"

The muzzle of a rifle appeared in front of her face in response. Jessica stared at the twisting blue current of the wormhole and judged her chances of getting past the gun.

"Don't try it. You don't have to be healthy, just alive. A few holes in your legs won't matter, in fact, it would keep you mighty contained."

Whoever he was, Jessica hated him in that second. Rage boiled through her as she was forced to back up towards the terminals and their crews of attendants. A line of soldiers lined the area with their automatic rifles aimed at her and Zeva as the Alcandian was dragged away from her world.

"Get the fuck away from my sister, Rinehart."

Cole pushed the gun out of her face but pulled her along with him as he moved out of the gate area.

"What just happened here, Cole?"

Cole flicked his eyes over the line of armed men and Rinehart before he charged through the doors and into the hallway.

"I don't know, but I'm going to find out, Sis."

Rinehart suddenly stepped into Cole's path and stared her brother in the eye with a grin. "The package is my responsibility. Feel free to take it up with York, but I keep the package."

Fingers curled around her biceps as Cole glared at Rinehart. He turned his head but the men behind her lifted their rifles as they tightened their grip on her body. Tension filled the air as Cole considered his targets. The men behind her tightened their grip again as they considered the fury burning on his face.

"Well, I'll just see what the hell York has to say, and if you even break one of my sister's fingernails, I'm going to break something a whole lot more important on your body."

Cole shot a warning at her escort and they lightened their grip instantly. "I'll be back, Sis."

"Well, it looks like I'll be waiting for you." Her voice dripped with sarcasm as she lamented not taking Zeva up on those lessons already. At least the men holding the Alcandian girl bore the marks of her ability to defend herself. They had only won by the sheer number of their ranks. Two of their number limped past on their way to the medical area for treatment.

Cole turned and moved down the hallway like a tornado. Raw violence dripped from his movements as Jessica was pulled towards another hallway and pushed through a door.

The room was only half-lit from some kind of ceiling lights and it was lined with mirrors. Jessica looked at the dark reflective walls and felt the eyes of someone watching her.

Zeva was pushed through the door hard enough to send her crashing to her knees. She sprang up from the floor in a second and rounded on the door. It slammed in her face as she gave a hiss of fury.

Jessica felt the walls press in on them with the very real fact that her brother might be flung into another cell and the keys to both doors melted down. Her stomach twisted into a knot as she thought about Jett returning to their room and an empty bed. She'd never told him that she wanted to stay.

And it was possible she might never get the chance to tell anyone that she wanted to go back to Alcandar.

# Chapter Nine

## ∞

"I owe you an apology." Zeva was leaning against the wall as Jessica stopped pacing the room.

"Great, you can teach me how to do that wrist lock thing you used on me. I wish you had taught it to me yesterday."

Zeva laughed as she looked at the door and then back at Jessica. The other girl was relaxed yet ready to spring into action the second that door even cracked.

"You're welcome at my studio anytime, but now we just have to get back to Alcandar for you to take me up on that invitation."

Zeva cast a long look at the mirrored walls and frowned. "That is if you are going back. I guess maybe you might get the chance to refuse to bind. What is it you say here...every curse is a blessing?"

"Maybe." And just possibly she was the biggest fool alive. Jessica frowned as she looked at their prison. The harsh words tossed in her face echoed across her mind as she considered Rinehart's view of her union with Jett and Dylan. Anger slowly burned a hole in her gut as she ached to get her hands wrapped around the soldier's neck. He had no idea that she'd found more honor in her ménage à trois relationship than she had even glimpsed in a date on Earth.

It went beyond sex and she knew that the soldiers guarding her were far too shallow to understand. Their weakness turned her stomach. The differences were stark. Dylan and Jett embodied the idea of men and the only fear she had was that she might never get the chance to tell them that.

"Yeah, maybe." Zeva suddenly relaxed against the wall as her eyes swam with contemplation.

"I expected better from you, Somerton." General York stared at Cole before he deliberately sat down, leaving the lower-ranking man on his feet in front of his desk. "Sometimes you need to plan a battle before engaging the enemy. We have what they want now and I fully intend to get that wormhole off my planet."

"You gave them your word, sir."

"That doesn't mean crap when it was given under duress. Those alien scum threatened to invade. Now, I've got them by the balls, son, and I'm not lightening the grip."

"You are talking about my sister."

"All that much better. Talk some sense into her. I bet she's relieved to be back on her home planet. My sister would be kissing my boots for rescuing her from that load of groupie sex kink they preach on that stinking planet."

Cole didn't say anything else. Instead he took a good look at what a superiority complex could do to an otherwise intelligent man. York was full of human pride and nothing was going to break through the wall of ignorance surrounding the man.

"Maybe you have a point, sir. I'd like to check in on Jessica. She might need some family support right now."

York folded his hands and raised an eyebrow. "I don't trust you, Somerton. You've turned alien-lover. Earth doesn't have any place for your kind. Want to see your sister? Fine, but she stays under guard until the Alcandians agree to let my man plant the charges that will destroy the gate."

Cole stepped back from the desk but stopped at the smile that spread across York's face. The General stood up and smirked at Cole.

"We'll have to give one of those women back to seal the deal but I can do my best to make sure it isn't your sister. No promises."

* * * * *

Jessica listened to her stomach grumble as a slit in the door opened and two trays were shoved into the room. Standing up, she picked them up and handed one food tray to Zeva before investigating her own. "It's food. Lousy food but better than nothing."

"Thanks, Jessica."

Zeva almost whispered her words. It was the first time she'd witnessed the girl look anything other than supremely confident. Her dark eyes simmered with doubt as she sat on the floor next to her.

"I guess Ravid will be furious right about now."

Zeva's eyes went round as she chewed on a piece of chicken experimentally. Jessica picked up the same thing from her tray and bit into it. "When you get home, maybe you should let the man try that mind-touching thing."

"I'm just not sure about Ravid." Zeva took a sip from her drinking glass before finishing her thought. "He is very strong, but I know he can be ruthless."

"Well, my mom says the only way to know a man is to love him."

"Really?" It sounded too risky. If either Keenan or Ravid touched her mind, there would be no escaping for her. Zeva knew in her heart the fever would ignite in that moment of contact. But Ravid was a judgment official. He imposed the penalties on other warriors who violated the law. The man went beyond ruthless — he was pure destruction.

Jessica watched the shiver that shook Zeva. The other woman hadn't seemed to be vulnerable before. Zeva certainly knew more about self-defense than she did. Yet, the two warriors chasing her caused almost the same reaction that she had to Dylan and Jett.

Maybe the decision to bind was far simpler than she was attempting to make it. Dylan's words floated across her memory — men were different than boys. The relationship between her and her mates would be different than the flirtation she'd shared with Bryan.

She had to be honest enough to admit that she didn't want Dylan or Jett any other way. She wanted men. In fact, she wanted her warriors.

Negotiating her relationships hadn't produced the kind of desire that Jett could summon up from her body. Playing nice with her on dates didn't give her the sense of strength that Dylan had always impacted her with.

Instead they were men who wouldn't make pretty excuses for what they felt for her. It didn't mean they couldn't be friends, but it did prove that she wasn't satisfied with pushover boyfriends.

Jessica actually felt her shoulders lift with that knowledge. Suddenly the future stretched out with endless possibilities. Marriage was a beginning in any culture. Brides and grooms were expected to give up their single-life habits and many times that included friends and homes.

Her heart contracted with bitter pain as she looked around her prison. The power of choice had been ripped away from her fingers. She had been so worried about being a possession that she'd never really noticed the difference in the way she'd been treated on Alcandar. Longing filled every cell in her body as she felt the minutes tick by like hours.

**\* \* \* \* \***

The door opened and Zeva shot to her feet. Cole was inside the room before she reached him. His eyes moved over each woman before he nodded his head. Jessica felt her blood freeze in her veins. She knew her brother too well. The look in his eyes was one of resolution.

"Earth has decided to end all contact with Alcandar."

"I thought it wasn't a choice."

"That would explain why they have taken hostages." Zeva glared at Cole before she shot Jessica a hard look. "Your people intend to use us as the seal on their agreement."

"They'll send you back, Zeva, just as soon as Alcandar promises to destroy the gate."

Cole didn't look at her and Jessica struggled to breathe. They were going to keep her. Hold Dylan and Jett to the agreement by separating them from their mate.

"I want to go back! Do you hear me, Cole? Tell your friends that I am going back too!"

\* \* \* \* \*

"Earth is not that important."

Dylan snarled but Jett placed a firm hand on his biceps. Warrior counsel was for open discussion. Every clan had representatives at the table and they were expected to speak their mind.

Ravid stood to be recognized. "I agree, but we must recover the two hostages. Any further contact can be postponed until a new gate can be constructed without the humans' knowledge. With their lack of advancement, it will be simple to hide a second gate. Invasion will cost lives."

There were many nods of agreement around the table. Dylan found the conversation grating on his patience. The need for battle surged through his body as he reached for Jessica and felt only a lingering essence of her. He was starving for her touch, thirsting for their mind-bridge. He clamped his control in place. Jett longed for a sister as well. His brother-at-arms should not have to remind him of the need for counsel.

"Any opposed?"

The table was silent. Dylan tossed a look at Ravid who summoned Keenan through their mind link. Keenan tossed an Earth solider into the chamber like a doll as he entered. The human smelled like his fear as he stuck his chest out and gripped his hands behind his back to hide their shaking.

"We accept your terms." The human smirked but the expression melted off his face as Keenan glared at him. An entire foot taller, the warrior tossed the man back out the door as Ravid joined him.

Dylan and Jett surged to their feet as the room emptied and they went towards the Earth gate. Jessica's face haunted his thoughts as he considered the fragile bargain Earth had offered. The humans had already broken their word by abducting their women. Each step towards the gate drove home the reality that Jessica might never set foot on Alcandar again.

They would rebuild the gate but it would take time and planning to place it on Earth without human detection. He would not survive the separation.

That was the only thing Dylan was certain of.

* * * * *

"Dinner's over. Let's go."

The lights suddenly surged to five times their level making Jessica squint as the door was opened. She was pulled to her feet as she struggled to make her eyes work. The hallway passed in a blur as she bounced between the hard bodies of soldiers. Sharp pinches on her bottom made her jump and collide with a different man who only smirked at her.

"Alien whore."

Zeva moved forward and linked arms with her as the group herded them towards the gate. Jessica looked at the pulsing current of blue like a desert mirage. Fifty feet separated her from it but it was the Grand Canyon with the rows of rifles pointed at her and Zeva. The men would cut their legs with bullets before either woman ever made it to the gate.

The wormhole popped and contorted as it opened. Jessica instantly felt Dylan as he stepped through the portal. General

York stepped forward as his solider moved away from Dylan at top speed. The man clicked his heels together before saluting the ranking officer.

"Charges set, sir!"

York smiled as he turned and flicked a hand at her and Zeva. Their escort parted and Jessica moved towards Dylan as she tightened her fingers on Zeva's arm.

"Move it! You've got twenty seconds before this gate is history. It was nice of Somerton to gather the data that helped us figure out how to blow their stinking wormhole into deep space."

"You're a lying bastard, York. You fucking used me."

"The men under my command are meant to be used. It's your Goddamned duty!"

"Jessica, come!"

Precious seconds remained. Jessica turned her head away from her brother as she moved towards the gate. She didn't know for a fact but she was quite sure that wormhole would explode just as York said it would. Her one and only chance to return to Dylan and Jett meant she would be leaving Cole behind.

She did it willingly. Her life was with Dylan and Jett.

Her arm was suddenly violently jerked. Her body went sideways as the returning solider jerked her against him. Zeva turned on one ankle and sent her leg smashing into the man's head. Jessica reached for her mates as she was pulled back by her clothing. Zeva gripped her wrist and yanked her out of the soldier's weak grip. She shoved Jessica towards the gate and sent a second kick at the soldier as he lunged after Jessica.

Jessica spun into Dylan and she knocked him back a step. It was only a single step but they were too close to the gate. Jett stood just inches behind Dylan and the gate sucked them into its current as they watched the soldiers converge on Zeva. She struggled against their bodies but they dragged her back as the blue current took over their vision.

They fell in a heap on Alcandar. Large warriors pulled them from the portal just seconds before the pulsing current exploded. Jessica reached back as she was pulled away, looking for any sign of Zeva. The entire building that housed the gate ignited from some unknown source as the Alcandian warriors watched it burn with solemn eyes. One by one they grinned at her and offered her short nods from their heads.

Her feet left the ground as Jett and Dylan smashed her between their chests. Her body rejoiced as she once again felt them inside her head and her heart filled up again with the joy they inspired. Reaching up she found Jett's head.

"I'm so sorry. Zeva pushed me."

"This is not your guilt to carry." Jett's voice was rich with rage as he dropped a kiss onto her neck. "The humans intended more deceit by keeping you." His dark eyes glittered as they sank into hers. "I confess I am overjoyed that you reached for us in that moment."

Dylan nuzzled her neck as Jett captured her lips in a kiss. Jessica yearned for her friend but couldn't help but kiss her mate back. She was home and it was far past time to bind.

\* \* \* \* \*

Sunlight streamed in and lit up the burgundy robe. Jessica stared at the garment as she fingered the sleeve.

Her stomach knotted with tension as she tried to unbutton her current clothing. She lifted her hand and giggled at the shaking fingers.

"Bridal jitters. Who would have guessed I could actually have them?"

A deep sigh came from behind her. Paneil was smiling so deeply her eyes turned into slits again. Lanai was nearly bursting with joy. The tide of elation wrapped her in its folds as she found the two women undoing her clothing for her.

Giggles and jokes sailed around the chamber as she bathed and dressed for her binding. It was a moment unbordered by culture or tradition. Male and female joined together all over the universe and the meaning was the same.

Unity.

Called marriage or binding, it meant the beginning of a new life.

# Chapter Ten
## ಬ

"Ravid, you are driving me insane." Jessica propped her hands onto her hips but she couldn't really find any true anger to aim at the warrior.

A large hand found the aching muscles of her back and began to rub. Dylan grunted as he listened to her sigh of pleasure. "You should not work so many hours, *heloni*."

"The waiting is driving me crazy, Dylan." Her son was three days overdue. The sight of her swollen belly in their chamber's mirror was enough to make her scream now.

"You make my heart burst, *heloni*." His hand stroked her belly as Jett joined them. His face turned gentle as he, too, rubbed her belly. Ravid watched them with heated eyes. The warrior had taken to watching her regularly. Rebuilding of the gate to Earth was progressing but not quickly enough to satisfy the man. He looked at her swollen belly and nodded before turning on his heel and leaving. Dylan sighed before pulling her closer to his large body. The sight of Keenan or Ravid always made them even more grateful for each other.

"I love you, too." And she did. It didn't make any sense. Jessica finally understood that it wasn't supposed to. Love struck without warning, it twisted and grew like a seed left behind in summer. One little season of rain and sun would transform that little capsule into a creation of life that would grow each and every year, until its branches were heavy and full.

Her son kicked as his fathers laughed in rich voices full of male pride.

Love, it could not be bound by laws or tradition. Instead, it emerged when the season called and stayed forever.

# About the Author

❧

I write to reassure myself that reality really is survivable. Between traffic jams and children's sporting schedules, there is romance lurking for anyone with the imagination to find it.

I spend my days making corsets and petticoats as a historical costumer. If you send me an invitation marked formal dress, you'd better give a date or I just might show up wearing my bustle.

I love to read a good romance and with the completion of my first novel, I've discovered I am addicted to writing these stories as well.

Dream big or you might never get beyond your front yard.

I love to hear what you think of my writing: Talk2MaryWine@hotmail.com.

Mary welcomes comments from readers. You can find her website and email address on her author bio page at www.ellorascave.com.

## Tell Us What You Think

We appreciate hearing reader opinions about our books. You can email us at Comments@EllorasCave.com.

# Why an electronic book?

We live in the Information Age—an exciting time in the history of human civilization, in which technology rules supreme and continues to progress in leaps and bounds every minute of every day. For a multitude of reasons, more and more avid literary fans are opting to purchase e-books instead of paper books. The question from those not yet initiated into the world of electronic reading is simply: *Why?*

1. *Price.* An electronic title at Ellora's Cave Publishing and Cerridwen Press runs anywhere from 40% to 75% less than the cover price of the exact same title in paperback format. Why? Basic mathematics and cost. It is less expensive to publish an e-book (no paper and printing, no warehousing and shipping) than it is to publish a paperback, so the savings are passed along to the consumer.

2. *Space.* Running out of room in your house for your books? That is one worry you will never have with electronic books. For a low one-time cost, you can purchase a handheld device specifically designed for e-reading. Many e-readers have large, convenient screens for viewing. Better yet, hundreds of titles can be stored within your new library—on a single microchip. There are a variety of e-readers from different manufacturers. You can also read e-books on your PC or laptop computer. (Please note that Ellora's Cave does not endorse any specific brands.

You can check our websites at www.ellorascave.com or www.cerridwenpress.com for information we make available to new consumers.)

3. *Mobility.* Because your new e-library consists of only a microchip within a small, easily transportable e-reader, your entire cache of books can be taken with you wherever you go.

4. *Personal Viewing Preferences.* Are the words you are currently reading too small? Too large? Too... ANNOYING? Paperback books cannot be modified according to personal preferences, but e-books can.

5. *Instant Gratification.* Is it the middle of the night and all the bookstores near you are closed? Are you tired of waiting days, sometimes weeks, for bookstores to ship the novels you bought? Ellora's Cave Publishing sells instantaneous downloads twenty-four hours a day, seven days a week, every day of the year. Our webstore is never closed. Our e-book delivery system is 100% automated, meaning your order is filled as soon as you pay for it.

Those are a few of the top reasons why electronic books are replacing paperbacks for many avid readers.

As always, Ellora's Cave and Cerridwen Press welcome your questions and comments. We invite you to email us at Comments@ellorascave.com or write to us directly at Ellora's Cave Publishing Inc., 1056 Home Avenue, Akron, OH 44310-3502.

erridwen, the Celtic Goddess of wisdom, was the muse who brought inspiration to storytellers and those in the creative arts. Cerridwen Press encompasses the best and most innovative stories in all genres of today's fiction. Visit our site and discover the newest titles by talented authors who still get inspired - much like the ancient storytellers did, once upon a time.

# Cerridwen Press
www.cerridwenpress.com

Discover for yourself why readers can't get enough
of the multiple award-winning publisher

Ellora's Cave.

Whether you prefer e-books or paperbacks,

be sure to visit EC on the web at
www.ellorascave.com

for an erotic reading experience that will leave you
breathless.

CPSIA information can be obtained at www.ICGtesting.com
Printed in the USA
BVOW08s1840310114

343636BV00001B/96/P